To Pat Lynch, my purple martin mentor, who has shown endless patience in helping me with this book and with my efforts to start a purple martin colony. Her untiring dedication to her own thriving martin colony qualifies her as a certifiable "wing nut."

WING NUT

CHAPTER
1

Grady Flood couldn't stand the heat of the flames on his face another second. He turned and slipped away from the group that circled the fire. Tonight was the Sunward Path Commune's first bonfire meeting of the year, which Grady knew meant at least a couple hours of boring discussion followed by endless singing. Now that it was April, the weekly meetings could be held outside, which was better than being crowded into the living room of the dilapidated farmhouse. Ever since he turned twelve a few months ago, Grady was considered an adult. He was required to attend meetings, but nobody could force him to listen.

The air was damp with dew as he walked through the darkness up the short driveway to the barn, just far enough away to let his mind wander without getting disapproving looks from the others. Grady settled on a bale of hay and leaned his tired back against the barn wall. He'd spent most of the day transplanting scrawny broccoli plants into the garden. Every muscle in his body ached, which didn't seem fair because he hated broccoli. But then, nothing at Sunward Path was fair.

"Wham! You're dead!" Grady was struck from the side, sending him sprawling on the ground. It was Tran, one of the younger commune boys. Tran was short for Tranquility, which Grady considered the worst case of misnaming a kid he had ever seen.

"I caught the monster," Tran crowed, pummeling Grady on the back. "Die, monster, die!"

Grady twisted around and captured the four-year-old in a hammerlock. "Hey, quiet down, Tran. You want to get us both in trouble?" Grady knew that was an empty threat. The little kids at Sunward Path couldn't get in trouble for anything short of murder, and even then, they'd probably get the benefit of the doubt.

Sunward Path was only one more in a series of dead-end places Grady and Lila had stayed since his father had died seven years ago. Grady had been five at the time. He did the math again in his head to make sure it was right. More than half of his life had been on the move, and the only thing that stayed constant was Lila.

He looked at his mother now, standing among the others. The orange firelight made her long wavy red hair look like it was flame itself. Grady was sure she could be a movie star if they could only make their way out to Hollywood. But Lila had never even tried to get them to California. Instead they had moved around through the Midwest, where she had slaved away at one low-paying job after another. Lila put up with a lot—more than Grady thought she should tolerate—but sooner or later something would get her upset enough to leave, and they'd pack up and take off without having a clue where they were headed.

Grady had a rating system for the places they stayed—ten for the best, one for the worst. Sunward Path was barely a three. They never had stayed at a one or two. A one would mean no food and no bed. Two would be either food or shelter, not both. But since Lila always looked for a job that would give them meals and a place to live, they had never sunk below the level of a three.

Tran wiggled loose from Grady's grip and ran off, but Grady knew he'd be back. There were six kids on the commune, ranging in age from two to seven, and they were pretty much allowed to roam at will. An outsider would have a hard time matching up the six kids with the fifteen adults. Since nobody else seemed to care, Grady had taken it upon himself to make sure none of the little guys got hurt. It wasn't an easy job, especially when he had chores to do. But the kids seemed to sense that Grady cared about them, and he usually had two or three of them following him around as if he were the Pied Piper.

Grady always felt it was his job to protect creatures smaller and more helpless than himself. Didn't matter if they were people or animals. His father had been like that. Anytime somebody found a starving stray dog or an injured wild animal they'd bring it to Arlan Flood. His dad once said he should put up a sign that read "When your car or animal stops running, bring it here. Whatever's broke, we'll fix it."

Grady liked the fact that he had inherited that talent from his father. Arlan Flood had been a big bear of a man, not exactly the kind you'd picture talking in a high little voice while he pulled a splinter from a dog's paw with tweezers, especially since his normal voice sounded more like the blast from an eighteen-wheeler's horn. It always seemed strange to Grady that Lila, who already had a soft, gentle voice, wasn't much good at animal saving. She had such a tender heart, all she ever could do was watch over his dad's shoulder and cry. Not that she was a softie all the time. When she got mad about something, she was like a terrier on a rat.

Grady noticed that the voices around the fire were raised in some sort of an argument, and Lila seemed to be right in the middle of it. He ran back to the group to find out what was going on.

"I can't do this no more," Lila was saying. In the firelight, her cheeks were shiny with tears. "When we first come here, everybody did their share, but now all the cooking and cleaning up falls to me. It's not fair."

Rayden, the commune leader, moved around the circle to put his arm across Lila's shoulders. "Lila, Lila, my dear child. You must understand that things have changed in the months you have been here. We used to be a group of workers, with only one or two philosophers, but now"—his arm gesture swept the circle—"philosophy has become our main focus."

Grady let out a little snort of disgust. Rayden had himself all dressed up to look like Jesus, if you could ignore his nose ring, the snake tattoo winding around his ankle, and the cell phone antenna sticking out of his burlap caftan pocket.

Rayden gave Grady a sharp look, then turned back to Lila. "We count on our group of workers to keep the community functioning to allow the others time for a higher purpose. Of course cooking and washing the dishes is every bit as important as finding the meaning of life, but we each must know our place and accept it." His little speech sounded like he was talking to someone Tran's age. Rayden smiled at the end to show everybody what a good guy he was. What a crock, Grady thought.

Grady heard the sharp intake of air that meant Lila was gearing up to let loose with her temper. Sure enough, Lila pushed Rayden's arm from her shoulders. "You know what, Rayden? You don't have no group of workers. You got me and Grady, and maybe one or two others, who work when the spirit moves them, which isn't very often. Only now you don't even have that, because Grady and me are getting out of here."

Grady squeezed in beside his mother, noticing that his shoulder was only a few inches lower than hers. In spite of the hard work, or maybe because of it, he'd grown a lot in the eight months they'd been here. He wedged himself firmly between Lila and the sweet-talking Rayden. Grady never had trusted that man. Something about Rayden's creepy smile and oily voice made the hairs stand up on the back of his neck. Grady's "crook, cheater, and no-good phony" radar had grown much sharper than his mother's, and he had pegged Rayden for all three right from the beginning.

The other commune members were whispering among themselves now. Tran and his little brother raced around inside the circle, playing tag. Not one of the adults stepped forward to keep the youngsters' bare feet from stepping on the hot coals that had rolled away from the edges of the fire. Grady grabbed the boys as they ran by, then deposited them in front of their mother. "You gotta take care of your kids," he said. "They could get hurt."

The young mother smiled dreamily. "Mother Earth takes care of her own."

"Well, Mother Earth is a lousy babysitter," Grady said, "because I been saving their hides at least a dozen times a day. You gotta watch 'em yerself from now on because I'm not gonna be here. They get in a lot of trouble when they're on their own."

Lila had left the circle and was headed toward the house. Grady ran to catch up, thinking how lucky he was to have a mother who had always looked after him. "You mean it, Mom, right? We're really taking off?"

"Oh, you bet I mean it." Lila's face was red, either from the heat of the fire or from anger. "They can do their high-and-mighty philosophizing all they want, but when their bellies are empty and the garbage and dirty dishes are piled up to the ceiling, maybe they'll wake up." Her voice bumped with each step as she slammed her heels into the ground. "Bunch of no-account snobs. Think they're smart just because their rich daddies sent them to college. I could teach every last one of them a thing or two about common sense."

Grady heard someone coming fast behind them in the dark. It was Russ, the new guy who'd been sniffing around Lila since the day he'd arrived about a month ago. He had come to Sunward Path to do research for a college paper comparing today's communes with the ones from the sixties or some darn fool thing like that. He was somebody else Grady didn't trust, but Lila was usually nice to him. Heck, she was nice to everybody until she saw through them. Russ caught her arm. "Lila, you aren't really thinking of leaving, are you?"

"Just watch me." Lila didn't break her stride.

"But where will you go?"

"Who knows? Anything's better than here."

Lila pushed the front door to the house so hard it smacked against the wall. Grady had to sidestep fast to keep from getting hit as the door bounced back. His mother was already up the stairs and into their room by the time he got into the house. As he reached their doorway, she tossed him his backpack. "Gather up all your stuff. We're leaving tonight. I wanna be out of here before those fools get back from the bonfire."

That wouldn't be hard. They hardly had any belongings to pack. Grady started scavenging under his bunk for stray socks. He only had five altogether, none of them mates. Heck, no two were even the same size. As Grady resurfaced from under the bed, he could hear the faint sound of singing coming up from the bonfire. Once the Sunward Path gang got started with the music, it could go on for hours. He and Lila would be long gone before anybody missed them.

Grady felt around the back edge of his mattress until he found the slit where he hid his two treasures—a worn-out paperback book and a little red Corvette. The two things he loved most in the world, next to his mother, were reading and cars. Not that he'd had much chance for reading here. The commune had an orange crate bookshelf with a few dusty old volumes on it, but as much as Grady tried, he couldn't make sense out of any of those books. So he read and reread his own book, discovering new things in the story each time.

"Don't be sitting there daydreaming," Lila said. "Let's go."

Grady stuffed the book and car into his backpack and took the stairs two at a time, trying to catch up with his mother. When he burst out into the damp night air, she was already in the car. Grady threw his pack into the backseat and slid in next to her.

"I sure hope they didn't run me out of gas," Lila said. Ever since Lila and Grady had arrived with their own car, the other commune members had been borrowing it to drive into town. First it was just once in a while. Then it was almost every day. Grady and Lila had both stopped noticing when it was taken, because nobody had bothered to ask permission for several months now.

Lila turned the key, but nothing happened. She banged her open palm against the steering wheel.

Grady started to get out. "No problem, Mom. I'll go siphon some gas out of the tractor."

Lila closed her eyes and leaned her head back on the seat. "It's not gas, Grady. The engine won't even turn over." She hit the steering wheel again. "How could I be so stupid? It's my car. I shoulda took better care of it. Your daddy always said you have to treat a car like a member of the family."

Russ knocked on the driver's-side window. "Your car has been on the fritz for a couple weeks now, Lila. Want me to take a look at it for you?"

"You know anything about engines, Russ?"

Russ shrugged. "I took a six-week mechanics course in junior high. It's not rocket science, you know."

"Okay, give it a try. We sure can't walk out of here." She slid over to make room for him.

Russ moved in close to her. "Maybe I could go along with you. Grady could use a father figure. Somebody to guide him on the path to becoming a man." He leaned forward over the steering wheel to grin at Grady.

Grady seethed with anger at that remark, as well as the one about auto mechanics not being rocket science. Grady's father had been the best mechanic in Mason County. Everybody had said so. And he had promised to teach Grady everything he knew, but then he died before he had a chance to do it. Grady would give anything to have his dad's mechanical skills, and now this jerk was making that sound like nothing. He got out of the car and closed the passenger door a lot harder than he needed to.

Lila gently pushed Russ away. "We'll talk about that later, Russ. Right now we got to get this car back on the road." She slid over to the passenger window. "We're not going anywhere tonight, Grady. Go on up to the room and get some sleep. Tomorrow's gonna be a big day."

"Why don't you come with me, Mom? You need sleep, too." Russ was trying to raise the hood. Grady glared at him. No way that jerk was going to be his dad.

"I'll stay and help Russ with the car." Lila got out and pulled their packs from the backseat. "Here, take my stuff up with yours." She pressed her forehead against Grady's and gave his arm a little squeeze as she handed him the bag.

"Mo-om," Grady whispered. "You gotta watch out for this guy. He's pure trouble."

"Russ'll give up on the car if I don't keep him working. I can take care of myself, Grady. Just you go in and leave me be."

Grady went up to the room, but he didn't even try to sleep. As much as he wanted to get away from Sunward Path, at least he knew how to deal with the people here. Whenever they moved on to a new place, Grady felt as if he and Lila were two cartoon characters accidentally running off the edge of a cliff. Lila was the lighthearted one who could do a double take, turn, and run through the air to land back on the cliff. Grady was the one who always felt the gravity of their situation. He dropped like a stone every time.

Grady ran his hand around the inside of the back-pack to find his book. It was so worn from reading, the edges of the pages were three times as thick as the spine. The book was about a girl named Gilly Hopkins who had been shipped around to a lot of foster homes, always hoping she'd end up with her mother. Grady had never been much for reading until he got that book. It was comforting to find another kid who was worse off than him, even if she was only a made-up character. Gilly wanted to be with her mother real bad. No matter how many times Grady got moved and no matter where he got shuffled to, he always had his mom right there with him. So that made him better off than Gilly.

The book had belonged to a library two doors down from where they lived when Lila worked as a waitress. The librarian had shown him lots of other books that were okay, but once he read *The Great Gilly Hopkins,* he kept taking it out over and over. One day, when he was checking it out again, the librarian said, "This book can't hold up to being taken out many more times, Grady." He went there so often, she knew his name. He knew her name, too— Mrs. Parravano. He liked the way it sounded like music when he said it. He had a sick feeling in his stomach that day. He didn't know what he would do if Mrs. Parravano wouldn't let him take out the book anymore. He *needed* that book, especially when he was plunging off that cliff. It kept him from hitting the bottom.

Mrs. Parravano had smiled at him. "Paperback books don't hold up as well as the hardcovers." She had taken it out of his hands. "You love this book so much, you should keep it. And I can show you lots of other books that you'll enjoy reading." Grady had held his breath, afraid he hadn't heard her right, but sure enough, she wrote DISCARD on the inside of the front cover and handed it to him.

He had clutched the book to his chest, too happy to find any words but "thank you," which didn't come anywhere close to the gratitude he was feeling. Nobody but Lila and his dad had ever given him a present. He didn't understand why Mrs. Parravano thought paperback books weren't as good as the ones with hard covers. A hardcover book seemed all stiff and serious, but an old familiar paperback was friendlier, fluffing up its pages like it was trying to open itself up to make you read it. Grady knew Gilly Hopkins so well, he could start on almost any page and jump right into the story without missing a beat, so he often set the book down on its spine and let the book choose the starting point for him.

Grady and Lila had moved away from that town a few days after Mrs. Parravano gave him his book. He never had a chance to say good-bye to the librarian. That was a shame, because he had thought of a better way to thank her. He wanted to say, "This book makes me feel safe," which was exactly right. But he probably would have been embarrassed to say that to her. And she might not have understood what he meant anyway, seeing as how she lived a pretty wonderful life, working in the library and all.

Grady stretched out on his lumpy cot and scrunched up the backpack to make a pillow. The book had opened to the part where Gilly was meeting a new kid in the foster home. The bare bulb hanging from the ceiling didn't throw enough light to read by, but Grady didn't need to see the words anymore to picture what was happening. He felt his breathing slow as he entered Gilly's world and played out the scene in his head.

He was distracted by a fly buzzing around the lightbulb. Then it zinged past his ear and hit the window screen, bouncing against it a few times with a metallic ping. Grady gently trapped the fly under his cupped hands, then slowly moved it to a hole in the screen, where it made its escape. "I'm getting away from here, too," he whispered, "first thing tomorrow morning."

Grady pivoted on his cot so he could lean on the windowsill, trying to hear what Lila and Russ were saying down below. The flames from the bonfire cast weird dancing shadows on the wall of the barn beyond. All Grady could make out was the low murmur of Lila's voice and the occasional clang of a wrench over a background of "Kumbaya." On about the thirty-seventh verse of "Kumbaya," he drifted off to sleep.

CHAPTER

2

When Grady woke up the next morning, the sky was barely tinged with pink. He was still in his clothes, stretched out full length on his cot with the windowsill digging into his cheek. He felt a sharp pain on the side of his neck as he slung the backpacks over his shoulder. When he got outside, Russ was working under the hood and Lila was behind the wheel.

Grady slid into the passenger seat and scrunched down so Russ wouldn't notice him. "He been working on this all night?"

Lila yawned and stretched. "No. Russ wanted to go back for the singing, so I slept in the car for a while. Then he wanted a nap, so he ain't been working on it more'n an hour or two. I think he's getting close, though. He's got it to turn over now, but it keeps stalling out." She ran her fingers over the indentation in Grady's cheek. "What did you do to yourself?"

Grady pulled away. "I slept wrong, is all. You don't look so good neither. You shoulda got more sleep."

She pinched the bridge of her nose—a sign that she had a headache. "I got some. Enough."

"That ought to hold her, Lila," Russ called. He came around to Grady's window. "If it starts cutting out on you again, make sure the hose is taped on tight to the carburetor. Grady, come here so I can show you this."

"I don't know nothing about engines," Grady mumbled, hoping Russ would let him alone. No such luck. Russ pulled the car door open so fast Grady almost fell out on the dirt driveway. "You don't need to know anything about engines. All you need to know is where to put the tape."

Grady looked back at his mother and asked a quick sign language question. "Is Russ coming with us?" It wasn't official sign language—just a way Grady and Lila had learned to communicate over the years when they were in a tight spot. It was done mostly with head tilts, shoulder shrugs, and eyebrows.

Lila's return gesture said, "No, he's not coming

with us. Let him show you about the car." A weight lifted from Grady's shoulders. He was almost cheerful, letting Russ explain about the hose.

"You got that, Grady?"

"Yeah, I got it. Russ, you sure are some kind of duct tape genius."

Russ looked pleased at Grady's false compliment. He smiled and ruffled Grady's hair in a fatherly gesture. Grady slipped away fast and got back in the car.

Russ slammed the hood closed and leaned down to Lila's window. "You sure you won't change your mind about me coming along? It isn't easy for a woman being alone on the road."

"She's not alone," Grady said, clenching his fist on the car seat.

Lila slipped her hand over Grady's. "We'll be fine, Russ. Thanks for your help."

Grady understood. No sense in having a fight with Russ now. It would only slow them down getting out of here.

Russ waggled his finger at Lila's dangly earring, making it send little sparkles of early morning sunlight over the dusty dashboard. "Well, if you change your mind about you and me getting together, you know where to find me." As he zeroed in to kiss Lila, Grady wished he had the button to close the window on Russ's neck. Darn thing didn't work anyway. Everything fancy on this car had worn out long ago.

Grady kept his eyes straight ahead as they backed out of the driveway.

Lila looked over at him. "The least you could do is wave good-bye, Grady. If Russ hadn't fixed the car for us, we wouldn't be going nowhere today."

"Russ don't know beans about cars. He's not Dad, you know. And I don't need a new dad, so don't be having a fool like Russ hang around with us on my account."

Grady said that to be mean—to see the way the corners of Lila's lips twitched down every time she thought of his dad, even after so much time had passed since the accident. He was sorry the second the words left his mouth. He didn't want to hurt his mother, but sometimes when he couldn't keep the edges of his world together, he took out his own panic on her.

If only Lila wasn't so darn pretty. Her red hair was real, not from a bottle, and her eyes were green— at least they looked that way when she was wearing her green sweater. She pulled guys in like flies on honey. She didn't even notice she was doing it, which made Grady nuts because he saw every look she got from men, and he knew what those looks meant. Grady wondered how long it took for a mom to get old and kind of ugly. It couldn't happen fast enough to suit him.

Lila fumbled in the compartment under the radio and fished out an old pair of sunglasses with only one ear wire. "I don't know why you'd think I'd let Russ take your father's place. Arlan Flood was my onliest ever true love. You get one of them in your whole lifetime, and some people never even find theirs. There ain't going to be nobody else, Grady. Only you and me."

Grady wished he could believe that, because they'd be fine, just the two of them. But there was always some guy wanting to butt in. And they all thought they had a perfect right to boss Grady around. Wherever they were going now, another Russ would be waiting to open the car door for Lila before she had turned off the engine.

Lila pulled out onto the main highway and picked up speed. "Here we go again, Grady. Off to a new life.

Look at that sign—'Welcome to Ohio'—like they knew we was coming."

Grady looked at the mirror in his visor and read the Welcome to Kentucky sign backward. He didn't care if he ever saw Kentucky again. He didn't care if he ever saw most of the places they'd been again. "Where are we headed this time?" He knew it must be east, because they were driving right into the sun. That seemed like a bad omen—another sunward path.

"How about New York?" Lila asked.

That got Grady's attention. "New York City? Doesn't it cost a lot to live there?"

"No, silly. Not the city. The state. New York for a New Life. Has a nice ring, don't it?"

"I guess. Long as you can find work."

This was the part that worried Grady every time. Lila always took off with no idea of how she could earn a living. In the past five years they had lived on two communes; three different houses where they had a room and Lila was a cook, a housekeeper, or both; and a room upstairs over a restaurant where Lila worked as a waitress for the room, tips, and all the food they could eat.

"We can't end up at a commune," Grady said. "I'd

starve before I'd go to another place like Sunward Path."

"They were mostly nice people, Grady, at least at first. And they taught us how to live off the land."

"Yeah, land that grew nothin' but broccoli and turnips!"

Lila smiled, knocking the one-eared glasses on an angle. "I think we were there the wrong time of year. If we'd stayed on until summer, there would have been tomatoes and squash and stuff."

Grady rolled his eyes. "Well, we better turn ourselves right around and go back there, because you didn't tell me I was missing out on squash."

Lila laughed and gave him a poke on the arm. "You wait. In a few days, we'll have a roof over our heads and all our meals for free. Don't I always find us somethin' good?" She started bobbing her head to the rhythm of a song on the radio, setting the earring sparkles in motion again and knocking the sunglasses almost clean off her face.

"You don't get nothin' for free, Mom. There's always a catch."

"Grady Flood, what makes you think that way? You can't believe something good will happen to us?"

She gave up on the broken sunglasses and tossed them into the backseat.

"I know you don't get something for nothing, is all. Things might look like they're free, but then after you get 'em, you have to pay somehow. Like the candy they gave me in that Bible school in Indiana, but then I had to listen to all that preaching stuff."

"A little preaching never hurt nobody. Probably better for you than the candy." She lifted her chin and stared straight at the road ahead. Grady could tell he had hurt her feelings again. Lila was an optimist, always looking for the best in everybody, which was why she ended up being friends with losers like Russ. She was always telling Grady things like "It don't cost you a penny to say a few kind words to a person who hasn't had the advantages we had." Grady couldn't for the life of him think of any advantages that had come their way so far.

They didn't talk much for the next couple of hours, just listened to the country-western stations Grady managed to tweak out of the static on the AM radio. They passed a Leaving Ohio, Come Back Soon sign and another one right away that said Entering Pennsylvania, followed by a whole lot of warnings about

what would happen if you were picked up for speed-
ing. Not much danger of that in their car, Grady
thought.

They were between radio stations, so Lila was
humming a happy song. Grady was caught halfway
between the excitement of going to a place that might
turn out to be the best place yet and the fear that it
could be the worst. Not knowing which kept him on
edge, but whatever it turned out to be, he knew he
could handle it. He had no choice but to make the best
of whatever he got.

They hadn't seen a town for quite a while when
the engine started to cough, then cut out at the top of
a hill.

"Oh, Lordy," Lila said, patting the dashboard.
"Don't give up on me now."

"Looks like your friend Russ used cheap tape."

Lila let the car roll as long as gravity kept it moving, then eased it over on the shoulder of the road.

"Go see what the problem is, honey."

Grady got out. He didn't have much faith in his
ability to get the car going again, so he looked around
for some signs of human life—maybe a farmer who
kept an ancient tractor running with chewing gum

and toothpicks. There was nothing here but a half-collapsed barn with a faded Mail Pouch Tobacco sign painted on its one vertical wall. Nearby an old chimney stuck up out of a crumbling stone foundation like an exclamation point. A cornfield with streaks of snow left unmelted in the purple shade between the rows stretched out as far as he could see.

Grady sighed and put up the hood, hoping for a sudden flash of genetic mechanical genius. Surely some of that would have been handed down from his father. Grady pulled the tape out of his pocket. He hadn't noticed before, but there were lots of hoses and most of them were taped up. There was a thick layer of black oil over everything.

Lila stuck her head out the window. "You see where it's come loose?"

"I'm checking it out." He wiggled one hose and it popped off, along with the one next to it. They were kind of springy, so he couldn't tell where they had been attached. Which thing was the carburetor? He should've paid more attention to Russ.

By now Lila was out of the car, looking over his shoulder. "We got two hoses loose?"

"Yep."

She leaned in close to the engine. "Well, can you tell where they come from? Because all you need to do is figure that out and tape them back on."

Grady just looked at her.

"Never mind," she said, squeezing his shoulder. "You woulda done that if you could figure it out, wouldn't you, sweetie? I wonder if we've still got the owner's manual in the glove compartment. They usually have little pictures that show how the engine should look."

"Don't matter how the engine should look, Mom. Those people at the commune drove this thing into the ground. It's not moving another inch, unless you got the money to get it towed and more money to get it fixed by somebody who *has* a clue."

"I don't have the money," Lila said. "Leastwise not enough for that."

Grady had figured as much, because when they had stopped at a gas station for lunch, Lila had to feel all around the corners of her purse to find the change to get them one can of Coke to split. He hoped she had a little emergency money tucked away somewhere—enough to get them to the next place. But the only money she made at the commune was from selling her baked goods to the neighbors, and she had to pay back part of that for the stuff she used from the commune kitchen. She couldn't have saved up much.

"Well," Lila said, "let's at least give it one last try. There's two hoses and two places to tape them to. We'll stick them on both ways. One's gotta work."

Grady taped the hoses, then Lila tried to start the car. Nothing. Then he switched the hoses and she tried again. The engine made some grinding noises. Then the grinding slowed down until it stopped. "Battery's dead now," Grady called.

Lila got out of the car and slammed the hood closed. She shaded her eyes from the bright spring sun and looked down the road in both directions. Grady leaned against the car and waited for her to decide what to do next. He sure didn't have any ideas. He marveled at how the brilliant sunshine didn't warm him even the slightest bit.

Lila finally opened the back door and tossed him his backpack.

"What? We're going to walk to New York?"

Lila slammed the door and shouldered her own pack. "Don't be silly. We'll walk until we get help. I'll find somebody. You know I will. I always do."

"But, Mom, we're in the middle of nowhere."

"Every place is somewhere, Grady. If you'd stop running your mouth and start running your feet, we'd be halfway there by now."

"Halfway where?"

"Anywhere!" she shouted over her shoulder. She didn't even look to see if Grady was following. She knew he would.

He always did.

CHAPTER

3

About an hour later, Grady was so cold his toes were numb. "Why couldn't we be doing this in June instead of April?"

"Because now is when we needed to leave," Lila said. "Anyways, I think I see a town up ahead."

She was right. There was a building. Didn't look like much, but Grady was ready to take anything with four walls and a roof. Heck, even three walls and a roof.

As they got closer to it, Grady's heart dropped. "It's only another old barn!"

"But look, Grady. There's something beyond. I think we're coming to a town."

Some town. There was a sign that said Welcome to Bedelia followed by four houses, a gas station, and a restaurant with a beat-up old trailer out back.

"Now isn't that lucky." Lila pulled herself up tall. "This town can provide me a position in an occupation with which I am already familiar."

When Lila was nervous, she started talking what she described as "fancy, like one of them college professors" to impress people. Grady hated when she did that. Sometimes when he could see people laughing behind Lila's back, he would glare at them until they got the message that it wasn't okay to make fun of her. Grady knew that Lila was smart in ways that didn't show on the outside. Phony talk kept people from seeing her the way she really was.

Lila stopped Grady at the door of the restaurant so she could comb through his hair and her own with her fingers before they went in. Her red wavy hair fell into place, while his straight brown hair slid right back over his forehead the second her fingers left it. He had his father's hair—"that slippery Flood hair," Lila called it.

When they went inside the restaurant, the first thing that hit Grady in the face was heat, which was surely welcome. That was followed by the smell of grease that had fried a few too many fish. He was so hungry, it made his mouth water.

The waitress behind the counter smiled as they entered. She was old, real old, but she had bright red lipstick and bright blue eye shadow. With her fish-white skin, Grady thought she looked like a greeting card for the Fourth of July. The name June was embroidered on her uniform pocket. "Sit yourselves down, folks. You took me by surprise. I didn't hear your car pull up."

Grady hitched himself onto one of the twirly stools, but Lila remained standing and reached out to shake June's hand. "Well, funny you should mention that, because that is a part of the predicament me and my offspring here, Grady, seem to find ourselves in. My name is Lila Flood, and my vee-hicle appears to have underwent some sort of a misfortunate occurrence."

Grady tried to shrink down into his jacket so the collar muffled the syrupy falseness of her voice.

The waitress leaned closer to Lila and squinted. "I'm sorry, dearie, but I can't make head nor tail of what you're trying to tell me."

Before June could mock her, Grady jumped in with, "Our car broke down. It's a piece of crap."

Lila gave him a look, then dialed her smile up a notch. "Please excuse my son's couthless behavior."

June laughed. "Not a problem, darlin'. I've heard much worse from the truck drivers passing through, believe me. Now, you're lucky to have landed here, because Sal Palvino across the street is probably the best mechanic for miles around. I'll give him a call and he can tow your car to his gas station. What's it look like?"

"It's mostly duct tape," Grady said. "The rest is rust."

June smiled and waggled a shiny red fingernail at Grady. "I like your sense of humor, kid." She reached for the phone on the wall.

Grady searched June's face for any sign of mockery, then relaxed a little. It was clear that June wasn't making fun of his mother. There wouldn't be any need to give her one of his dark looks.

"Wait, June," Lila said. "I can't have the car fixed. Leastwise not right now. I gotta work awhile first. Save up some, you know?" Lila was talking like her normal self now, and June seemed nice—the kind of person who might be able to help them. On a scale of one to ten, this place was already up to a five.

June put the phone back on the hook. "Okay. I catch your drift. You got somethin' lined up, honey?"

"Well, we're headed for New York."

June raised her eyebrows. They were just drawn in black pencil, no hairs. "You got yourself a job in the Big Apple?"

"No. We're going to the state. Not the city."

"Well, that's good, too, sweetie, but you're at least fifty miles from the New York State line. How are you getting to New York with no car?"

Lila sat down at the counter. "That's the problem. I was hoping maybe you might have something for me here. I'm a good waitress and a hard worker. I got experience and all."

Grady twirled his seat so his back was to them and turtled his neck down into the collar. This was the part he hated most, when Lila had to beg for a job. Not that she wasn't good at it, because she always got work. But it made him feel crummy all the same, as if they weren't as good as other folks.

"Look," June said. "I'd give you a job if I could, but you can see we're not exactly runnin' over with customers here. Ever since they opened up the new section of the turnpike, all we get are the people who are too cheap to pay the toll."

Yeah, well, that would be us, Grady thought. No way Lila would spend good money to drive on any darn road.

Lila stood and shouldered her backpack. "Don't you trouble yourself none about us, June. Thanks anyway. Sorry to have bothered you. C'mon, Grady. We gotta get going."

Grady must have shown the sudden panic he felt, because June caught Lila's sleeve. "No, wait, honey. We'll think of something. Sit down and have a bite to eat. We'll figure this out."

Lila turned around and slid in beside Grady. "I want you to know I don't take no charity. I work for my keep."

"Don't worry about it. The meat loaf and mashed potatoes haven't been too popular today. You'd be doing us a favor if you'd take them off our hands. Mashed potatoes don't keep, and the meat loaf was from Sunday."

"I guess we could do that," Lila said. "I mean if you were going to throw it out."

June disappeared into the kitchen and came back with two plates of food. Grady almost swallowed that hunk of meat loaf without chewing. It was that good. Or he was that hungry.

June poured Grady a glass of milk, then coffee for Lila and herself. "You think you might have enough money for bus tickets? There's no bus going through here, but I could give you a lift over to the station at Addieville. Depending on where you're going in New York, it probably wouldn't be more than forty dollars for you, maybe fifteen, twenty for the kid." She looked at Grady. "You're not twelve yet, are you?"

Grady's mouth was full, so he nodded.

June shrugged. "That's all right. You'll slouch a little. So we're talking fifty-five, maybe sixty. You got that much, dearie?"

Lila held her coffee cup in both hands, hunching as if she were warming herself over a campfire. "No, not that much. Not even close."

"Well, if I had it, I'd loan it to you myself. I'm always doing darn fool things like that. If I had every dime I ever loaned to a complete stranger with a good story, I'd be a rich woman."

"That's the Lord's own truth." An old guy with a grease-stained apron had come out of the kitchen.

June tilted her head toward him. "That's Bob, my husband. You been eavesdropping on Lila and me?"

He switched the toothpick he was chewing to the opposite corner of his mouth. "Don't I always? How else would I keep those truckers from running off with my beautiful wife?" He smiled, leaving the tooth-pick balanced on his bottom teeth.

"So you got any ideas?" June asked.

Bob leaned on the counter in front of Lila. "You need to have a car where you're going?"

"Well, I'm used to having my car"—Lila bit her lip and thought for a minute—"but I guess I could manage without it. Depends on where we end up."

"Maybe Sal would buy it, then," Bob said. "That would give you the money for bus tickets."

June patted him on the head. "Bob, you may look dumb as a doorknob, but your poor old brain is still breathing in there." She grabbed the phone and punched in the numbers. "Sal? June. I got a customer here. . . . Yeah, yeah, very funny . . . I got a customer here who might want to sell her car. . . . No, she can't bring it in. It's stalled down the road." She turned to Lila. "Which direction?"

Lila pointed.

"Out toward Hester. Can't be too far. They walked in from there. Okay, thanks, Sal. Stop by after you take a look-see. I got some peach pie left." She laughed. "You know it, baby. Thanks!" She hung up the phone. "He's going right now to check it out. He'll give you a fair price."

June cut two big pieces of peach pie.

Lila pushed the plate away. "I can't let you give us that, June. There's no way you were throwing out that pie."

What was she doing? Grady hadn't had a piece of pie for months. He hunkered down and curved his arm around his plate so Lila couldn't get at it.

June winked at Grady and pushed Lila's plate back at her. "You can't have a meal without something sweet at the end, Lila. It's a rule around here."

Lila picked up her fork. "Well, I wouldn't want to go breaking rules, but I'll do some work for you in return."

Grady took a big bite of the pie. It had a crust so flaky it practically fell apart when he touched it with his fork. Man, he never tasted anything like it. When he finished the pie, Grady licked his finger and used it to pick up every last little flake of crust on the plate.

June poured Grady some more milk. "You liked that, did you, Grady?"

"Yes, ma'am. That's about the best pie I ever tasted."

"Don't be telling her that," Bob said. "She'll want me to pay her more money."

Lila was already working without June telling her what to do. First she swept the floor. Then she gathered up all the napkin holders and filled them from the big pack of napkins behind the counter.

Grady finished his second glass of milk, then ducked out to use the restroom behind the building before Lila got the idea of him working for his pie, too.

Before he went back in, Grady looked around to see if maybe he had missed seeing part of the town before. He hadn't. There was nothing here. Even Sunward Path had more buildings than this place. June and Bob should move their restaurant to a bigger town if they didn't want to be throwing out their meat loaf every day. Anybody could see there weren't enough customers here to keep the place in business. Not a car or truck coming or going as far as the eye could see.

So there was no work for Lila here, and Grady couldn't see what good it would do to take a bus into New York. What if they used up all their money on the bus fare and didn't find work there, either? He wished Lila would worry more about things like that so it didn't all fall on his shoulders.

By the time Grady got back inside, Lila was laughing and carrying on with Bob and June as if they'd all gone to high school together, even though Bob and June were about a hundred years older than her. Lila was finishing up filling the sugar bowls when the door opened and a guy came in. He was tall and good looking with dark hair that hung over one eyebrow like Elvis Presley. He should've had the word *trouble* tattooed across his forehead. "Hey, Sal," June said. "Take a load off your feet and tell us what you think of the car."

Sal slid onto the stool next to Lila and gave her a grin. Grady got a prickly feeling on the back of his neck. So here was the next Russ. And they weren't even in New York yet.

CHAPTER
4

June poured Sal a cup of coffee. He put four spoons of sugar in it. Grady was almost hypnotized watching him stir. Sal finally put down the spoon and looked up at Lila, smiling to show off his movie star teeth. He even had a dimple in one cheek. Why did they have to keep running into guys like this? "I have one question for you," Sal said. "What did you do with the horse?"

"What horse?" Lila asked.

"The horse you used to tow that car, because there's no way that heap got here on its own. Whoever worked on it last was clueless."

"It got here just fine," Grady said. Oh, great. Now he was defending Russ's mechanical skills to the new Russ.

"Look, kid. I'm not trying to insult your car. It's a miracle that you got here, that's all."

"So you can't give me any money for it?" Lila asked. "I was hoping for enough to get bus tickets to New York."

Sal tried to sip the coffee, but it was too hot. He wiped his mouth with the back of his hand. "Sorry, but I'd have to spend a fortune to repair that car, and then there's no guarantee I could actually get it running again. I don't have any use for a car I can't fix. Besides, it's got too much rust on it. Nobody would pay me enough money for it to cover the parts."

"Can't you use some of the good parts, Sal?" June slid a piece of pie across the counter to him. "Couldn't you pull about seventy, eighty bucks' worth of stuff off it?"

"June, I'd like to help you out, but the whole thing's held together with duct tape. There's not a decent part to be had."

"That's okay," Lila said. "If you can't, you can't. Thanks for looking at it, though."

Sal ducked his head and smiled. "My pleasure." Then he looked at Lila from under that lock of Elvis hair. The *trouble* tattoo had turned into a flashing neon sign.

Suddenly June smacked herself on the head. "Why didn't I think of this before? Roger and Ethel Fernwald

were in here for dinner the other night. They're moving to Florida and they want to find someone to take
care of Roger's dad, Charlie. He won't sell the farm,
but they're afraid to have him living out there all
alone."

Bob laughed. "Hoo, boy! Old Charlie Fernwald?
Did he agree to having a babysitter?"

"I don't think he has anything to say about it.
Roger is doing the hiring. Charlie does get to pick the
person, though."

"Isn't Charlie Fernwald that crazy old guy up on
Wheeler Hill?" Sal asked.

June piled the dishes and put them in the sink.
"He's not crazy. Maybe a little—what do they call it?
Eccentric." She turned back to Lila. "What do you
think, honey? There's a nice little cottage on the farm
for the caretaker."

Lila perked right up at that. "Really? We'd have
our own house?"

Grady knew those were magic words. He and Lila
hadn't lived in their own house since the accident. Lila's
dream was to have a real home again. He'd never get
her away from here if they got their own place.

"You'd get all your meals, too," June said, "and

some pay. You'd have to do the cleaning and cooking, laundry and such, if I remember right. You could do it until you had the money to move on. I wouldn't tell Roger that, though. He wants somebody permanent. But with Charlie Fernwald, nobody's likely to last more than a month or so."

"Well, there's really no reason we have to go to New York right away," Lila said. "Sometimes a good opportunity just drops into your lap. Right, Grady?"

He avoided looking at his mother. He knew she'd have that old "see, I told you" look on her face.

Bob wiped the counter with a wet rag. "If I was you, I'd meet old Charlie Fernwald before I started making any plans, because he's not exactly what I'd call a good opportunity. You'll have your hands full with that one."

"Well, I don't want to go bragging' on myself," Lila said, "but I have a way with people. I bet that old gentleman and me will get along fine. How can I get to meet him?"

Sal stood up. "I'll take you out there, Lila. I have a kid watching the station for me."

"Hey, hold on a minute," June said. "Charlie don't

47

like surprises. Let me give him a call and ask if you can come over."

"Why give him a chance to say no?" Sal said. "We'll head out right now." He helped Lila on with her jacket, and they started for the door. Grady picked up the backpacks and followed. Why was this guy in such an all-fired hurry?

"I'm going to call Roger, too," June said. "He can meet you there. Might smooth things over a bit."

When they got to his pickup truck, Sal looked surprised to see Grady. "Oh, yeah, kid. Sorry. You can go, too." He took the backpacks from Grady and tossed them into the truck bed. Lila started to get in, but Grady squeezed ahead and plunked himself in the middle of the seat—right between his mother and trouble.

A few miles down the road, they went through a town. It wasn't much, but at least it had some stores, a couple of churches, and a bunch of houses. Grady had his eye out for a library but didn't see one. Of course it could have been hidden down a side street.

Sal drove past an empty parking lot with a big school

building. Grady read a sign that said Melvin Proctor Junior-Senior High School and felt his meat loaf roll around in his stomach.

"The school looks closed," Lila said. "Is this some sort of holiday?"

"It's closed for good," Sal said. "Now they bus all the kids from seventh grade up over to Addieville. It's a big central school."

School was the worst part of moving to a new place. The first day he stepped into a new school, it was like diving into a tank of freezing water. Grady wondered what names he'd be called here. Maybe he'd be lucky this time. Maybe he'd dive into that tank of water and drown right then and there. Or maybe he'd be even luckier and they'd move on before anybody tried to make him go to school.

"Grady?" Lila had been saying something to him. "Huh?"

"Sal says there's a nice big central school here."

"That's great, Mom." Maybe if it was big, he could be invisible. Although he had been in big schools before. Nobody ever had any trouble figuring out that he was the weird new kid and zeroing in on him.

"You should see the gym in that place," Sal said.

"They have the best ath-a-letic program in ten counties. People from all around here go to the games, whether they got kids or not. What are you in, kid, about seventh grade?"

Grady nodded, not that it was any of Sal's business.

"Well, then you could play junior varsity baseball. The season just started a few weeks ago. Addieville's team came in second in state regionals last year."

Great. There was nothing Grady hated more than going to school with a bunch of jocks. At least on the communes all the kids were oddballs and you could score points by being good at folk dancing or weaving cane chair seats.

Sal gunned the engine as they started up a steep hill. "That's Charlie Fernwald's place up there."

There was a big old farmhouse, a couple of barns, and what looked like a kids' playhouse off under some trees. There were no other houses in sight. As they pulled into the long driveway, an old man came down off the porch. The way he was marching toward them, Grady was sure he was coming to run them off his property.

They barely got out of the truck before the old guy started in. "You the folks June called about?"

"Yes, sir," Lila said with her biggest smile. She held out her hand. "I'm Lila Flood, and I'm delighted to be applying for the position of being your personal assistant. My spe-shee-ality is making a gracious and healthifying home for those of the elder persuasion." When Charlie didn't shake her hand, Lila let hers fall to her side, but her smile got even brighter and phonier.

Grady groaned inside at Lila's fancy language.

It was pretty obvious that Mr. Charlie Fernwald wasn't impressed one single bit by Lila's act. "Whatever it is you do, young lady, I'm sure you're real good at it. But you're just not going to do it here, because I have not as yet been persuaded to be elder. So if you'll all climb back into that truck, I have things to do."

He turned and started walking away. That's when Lila caught sight of the small house. Now that they were close up, Grady could see that it wasn't a kids' playhouse. It was a real cottage. It even had a front porch with two rocking chairs. Lila had a thing for porches. "Oh, Grady, look," she whispered. "There's the little house. Isn't that the cutest thing you ever saw?"

"Mom, the guy doesn't want us here."

Lila lifted her chin. "Oh, he will, Grady. You wait.

He will." She ran after Charlie Fernwald and caught up to him on the porch of the big house. Grady followed slowly. He wanted to be nearby in case Charlie was mean to Lila. Sal didn't seem to care about that. He leaned against the side of the truck and lit a cigarette.

As Grady got closer, he heard Lila say, "If you would give me a chance to demonstrate my kitchen skills, Mr. Fernwald, I'm sure you would discover that I'm an excellent chef."

"I'm sure you are, but I've been feeding myself ever since my wife died, which is four years now. I don't look like I'm starving, do I?"

He sure didn't. There was definite evidence of a potbelly under his farmer's overalls. He was mostly bald on top with a fringe of hair over his ears, but he looked pretty strong for an old guy. He had freckles on his face and all the way over his bald head. His hair hadn't turned gray or white the way most old geezers' did. It looked like red hair that had faded, like an old blanket that had been washed so many times, most of the color had come out of it.

Charlie finally noticed Grady. "Is this your kid?"

"Yes, sir. This is my offspring, Grady."

Lila nudged Grady, so he held out his hand and Charlie shook it.

"Well, nice to meet you both, but even if I wanted help here—which I definitely don't—there's no room for two people in that cottage. It's barely big enough for one."

"Oh, Grady and me is used to fitting in small places," Lila said. "We've never had nothing so nice as this." She put her hand to her mouth, realizing she had dropped her fancy talk and given away the fact that they were nobody special.

Charlie lifted his chin so he could look at them through the bottom part of his glasses. "All right, what's your deal? You're not one of those aides Roger keeps sending out from the agency, because June at the restaurant is the one who called me. So you're just passing through here? Is that it?"

"We would have passed through if our car hadn't died," Grady said.

Charlie shaded his eyes to see Sal standing by the truck. "Now this is starting to make some sense. That's the guy with the gas station out by June's place. You just need a place to stay while the car is being fixed?"

"Oh, no," Lila said. "I'm looking for a permanent position."

That's when Grady thought he got the picture.

Charlie didn't want a permanent person. He just needed to look like he had one until his son moved away. Grady decided to use the honest approach, since Lila's professor act hadn't worked. "Mom needs to earn enough to get a new car. Well, not a new one. A used one that runs good. Then we'll be moving on. So we won't be around here all that long."

Lila gave Grady a poke in the ribs, but he could tell by the change in Charlie's expression that he was on the right track. Besides, he and Lila had to have somewhere to live until they could get out of there, and he was pretty sure Sal might be offering to have them bunk in with him. No way Grady was going to let that happen.

Charlie rubbed his chin. "This might not be so bad. My son and his wife are moving in two weeks. Long as they think I have somebody, they'll leave me alone. You could stay here until you had enough money for the car. By then Roger would be long gone."

"But you would let me cook and clean for you, wouldn't you?" Lila asked. "I wouldn't feel right about taking money for doing nothing. I don't ever take no charity."

Charlie didn't get a chance to answer, because a car came into the driveway so fast it was spitting gravel behind it. "Here's my son now. Let me handle this. We'll work things out after he leaves."

A guy got out of the car and ran toward the house. "Don't make any snap judgments, Dad," he called out. "Let's talk this over."

"There's nothing to talk over, Roger."

Roger bounded up onto the porch. "But, Dad, you've turned down so many applicants."

"I know. That's why I'm hiring this woman."

Lila gave a little gasp and squeezed Grady's hand.

"Well, now, that's wonderful." Roger turned and gave Lila and Grady a once-over. "Does she have any references?"

Grady folded his arms to hide the ripped cuff on his jacket.

"You think I've taken leave of my senses?" Charlie asked. "You think I'm going to hire some complete stranger who drops in out of nowhere without checking on her references?"

"Well, no, of course not, Dad. I didn't mean to imply . . ."

"Just remember I've given you every bit of common

sense you have, Roger. Many's the time I've saved you from being bamboozled by some con artist over the years. Isn't that right?"

Roger looked like a scolded puppy. He mumbled something Grady couldn't hear.

Charlie turned to Lila. "Now, when did you say you could start?"

Lila clapped. Grady hoped she wouldn't go into her happy dance and blow the whole deal. "I can start this very minute."

Roger looked a bit uneasy, but smiled and patted his father on the back. "Well, then, I guess it's settled, Dad."

Grady left them to work out the arrangements. He ran down the driveway and pulled their backpacks out of the truck bed.

Sal ground out the cigarette with the heel of his boot. "So she got the job?"

"Yep."

He looked past Grady at Lila. "Guess I'll be seeing a lot of you folks from now on." That neon sign was flashing like a beacon.

"I don't think so," Grady said. "The old goat says we can't have anybody come around here. Says he chases people off with a gun. I'd stay away if I was you."

As Grady lugged their backpacks up to the house, he could hear the truck spin its wheels going out of the driveway.

Good-bye, Russ number two.

CHAPTER
5

Grady waited on the porch of the little house for Lila to come back. He tried to peek inside, but there were curtains pulled shut across the windows. The whole house was only half the size of a small trailer. Grady put down the backpacks and sat in one of the rocking chairs. The cottage was right at the top of a hill. Grady could see for a long distance, but there was nothing much to look at. The only signs of life were barns with silos and a small herd of cows dotting the distant landscape. For once Grady hoped Lila would get fed up with her job quick, because it didn't look as if there was much to hang around for. If she could earn them enough money to get a set of wheels, they could move on to someplace more exciting.

Charlie's old farmhouse was white with green shutters. Behind it was a big red barn with a silo. If there were snow on the ground, it would look almost exactly like the country Christmas card Lila always taped to the wall over her bed when they moved to a new place. Grady had once asked her if it reminded her of home. She told him it looked like the place she'd like to live someday. And now here it was in real life, in plain view from her front porch. Grady could have a hard time getting her to leave here.

The only things that caught Grady's interest were the three tall TV antennas in the big open yard in front of Charlie's porch. At least they should get some pretty good reception with all that fancy equipment. Maybe life on Charlie's farm wouldn't be totally boring after all. There sure hadn't been any TV on the commune. No radio, either.

A couple of car doors slammed, then Charlie's son and his wife drove past the cottage. Grady could see Lila and Charlie heading his way. Lila looked like a little kid all set to open a big pile of birthday presents. If she walked any bouncier, she'd be skipping.

Charlie Fernwald pulled some keys out of his pocket as they came up on the porch. "This one is for the front door. The smaller one is for the back. You don't need to use them, though. Around here we leave things unlocked, unless you're hiding some diamonds in those backpacks."

"Oh, no," Lila said. "I don't have nothing like diamonds. Only the one little rhinestone tennis bracelet I got from the five-and-dime is all, and I got that on clearance. I never played tennis, but I thought the bracelet was pretty."

Grady wished Lila could tell when somebody was making a joke. He saw Charlie shake his head and smile. Grady glared at him so he'd know it wasn't okay to make fun of her.

The door stuck at first, but Charlie pounded it with his fist and it opened. Grady followed them inside, dragging the backpacks. It was one small room with two doors and another doorway covered by a curtain. He could see that the one led outside in the back. He couldn't figure out what the other two were until Charlie opened one. "Here's your bathroom. There's no tub, but the shower works." He pulled back the curtain. "This is a good-sized closet." Charlie eyed their pitiful pile of belongings. "If you don't have too much to store, you could put a cot in here and call it a second bedroom." He pulled a string to turn on the bare lightbulb that hung from the ceiling.

Grady leaned past him and looked inside. A cot would fill that room from wall to wall. The swinging light made the little red flowers on the peeling wallpaper look like ladybugs crawling across the walls. "Where's the first bedroom?" Grady asked.

"Right here." Charlie walked across the room and grabbed a handle on the wall. A bed pulled down, barely clearing the old couch and stuffed chair. They all had to squeeze against the wall to make room for it. "Murphy bed," Charlie explained. "Pulls up out of the way when you don't need it." He lifted it back in place and went over to a corner where there was a small stove, refrigerator, and sink. Charlie tugged another handle and a piece of the wall pivoted up to become a table, its legs folding out from somewhere underneath. The table filled about half of the room.

"What if one of us wants to eat and the other one wants to sleep at the same time?" Grady asked.

"Guess you'd be out of luck," Charlie said. "I told you it was small. I built it as a playhouse when our kids were little. Then my wife had me add the bed and kitchen so it could be a guesthouse. If you don't think it's big enough, you can be on your way."

"Oh, it's plenty of room," Lila said. "We'll manage fine here, Mr. Fernwald. Don't you worry none about that."

"All right, then. If you send the boy up to the house, I'll get the cot out for him."

"My name is Grady." If Lila had been paying attention, Grady would have felt her elbow in his ribs for that remark. She was running her fingers over the table with a dreamy look in her eyes.

Charlie stopped at the door and turned to look at Grady. "Fair enough. Grady. That your first name or your last name?"

"First name."

He nodded. "Funny, you don't run into any Bobs, Bills, or Marys anymore. Seems like everybody's got to be a Cody or a Crosby or a Madison. Kids today have their names on backwards, if you ask me."

"Nobody asked you," Grady mumbled.

"What's that?"

"I said I'll come right after you. To the house, I mean. For the cot."

Charlie's eyes narrowed. "Uh-huh. Give me about

fifteen minutes to find it. I'll leave it out on the porch for you."

When Charlie let the screen door slam behind him, Lila woke up from her daydream and ran out onto the porch. "Oh, Mr. Fernwald, what time do you want me to come up and cook your dinner?"

"I don't need anybody cooking for me. I have a whole freezer full of dinners. Salisbury steak with french fries. Have it twice a day. Some days three times, if I run out of Sugar Loops."

Lila kicked into high gear with her healthy food speech—propaganda from their first commune. "But that's not good for you, Mr. Fernwald. You should have some nice fresh vegetables. Maybe a salad."

Charlie Fernwald came back and took hold of the porch railing. "Look, Lisa, I'm sure you mean well."

"Lila," Grady corrected.

Charlie cleared his throat. "Lila. I'm going to tell it to you real nice and clear. My mama died over forty years ago and I haven't eaten a vegetable since. Even my dear departed wife couldn't make me eat any rabbit food, so forget about it. I'll see you in the morning."

Lila came back into the house and dropped down on the couch. A little cloud of dust came out of it when she landed. "Grady, I do believe I was sent here for a purpose. It wasn't no accident, that car breaking down where it did."

"Of course it wasn't no accident," Grady said. "Russ made it happen because he's an idiot. Any fool knows a car won't run on duct tape."

"No, really. Come here and listen to me." She patted the cushion next to her, raising up another puff of dust. "Grady, I'm having a vision clear as anything."

Lila was always having visions. She was always seeing into the future, only the future she was seeing was never anything like the future that really happened. "Grady, I have been sent here to save that man."

"Save who? Charlie Fernwald?"

"Yes. That man is killing himself with all that bad food he's eating, and I'm going to rescue him."

"How can he be killing himself? He's got to be about a hundred years old. Besides, anybody that mean will live forever, even if he don't eat nothing but pork rinds dipped in hog grease."

All the talk about food was making Grady hungry. He got up to check out the fridge. It was empty except for a box of baking soda, which didn't look like anything you'd want to eat. He opened all the little cupboards over the sink. There were some dishes and glasses and a couple of pots and pans. No food. "What are we supposed to eat here? Maybe the old geezer is all set with his frozen stuff, but there's nothing for us. I'll ask him if we can have a couple of those sauce-berry steak things."

"You won't ask any such thing, Grady. We had a good lunch. We don't need no more than one big meal a day. I'm still full."

"Well, I'm not! Jeez, Mom, you're always bugging me about how a growing boy has to have his three squares a day. What happened to *that* rule all of a sudden?"

"I'm sure we'll get this all straightened out in the morning. I don't want to give that man no reason to send us away before I even get a chance to work my magic on him."

"Magic! How about waving your magic wand and giving your son a meal before he starves to death?"

"You'll live, Grady. Make yourself useful and run on up to the house to get that cot. Otherwise you'll be sleeping on the floor tonight. Then you'll have something to complain about."

"I got another thing to complain about. That guy has all those TV antennas outside, but do you see a TV in here? Would it kill him to give us one tiny TV?"

"What's got into you? We never had a TV, except for that room over the restaurant. Seems to me you can manage perfectly well without a TV."

"Fine!" Grady slammed out the door and headed for the big house. He found the cot on the porch, but he didn't stop there. Through the front window he could see Charlie Fernwald sitting on his couch, eating a dinner out of a little cardboard box with a plastic spoon. He knocked on the door.

It took Charlie a few minutes to get up and come over. "Didn't you see the cot? I put it over by the steps. There's a pile of bedding next to it. Let me know if you need an extra quilt. I got plenty."

"You should let my mother make meals for you," Grady said. "She's a great cook."

"I'm sure she is, but I don't need a cook. You can stay in the house, though. Long as you keep out of my hair, I don't care what you do. All I ask is that you leave the place the way you found it. "

He started to close the door, but Grady stuck out his

foot to block it. "Hey, wait a minute. We got another problem here. Meals were supposed to come with this job. If Mom doesn't cook for you, how do we get anything to eat?"

Charlie rubbed his forehead. "Hadn't thought about that. All right." He dug around in the pocket of his overalls and pulled out a wrinkled twenty-dollar bill. "Here, take this and get some food for yourselves."

"Where's the grocery store?"

"Where do you think it would be? Down in town."

"Well, how are we supposed to get there? We don't have a car, and it's too far to walk." Grady was afraid Charlie would say he had to walk twice as far when he was a kid. That's what old people always did—brag about how much harder they had it when they were kids, walking through blizzards up mountains to school. Who did they think they were fooling? No way any kid would work *that* hard to get to school.

Charlie held out some keys, but he hung on to them a little too tight for Grady to take them. "Is your mother a good driver?"

"She is when she's not trying to drive some piece of junk."

Charlie looked at him hard, then let go of the keys. "I must be crazy, because I don't know either one of you from Adam, but I can't let you starve. My truck is in the barn. Go get what you need from town. I'm calling Sheriff Halloren so he knows it's all right for you to be driving the truck."

Charlie caught Grady's arm as he started for the door. "The sheriff is a good friend of mine, so don't get any ideas about leaving town. He'll have his eye out for you one way or the other."

Grady wanted to throw the keys back in his face, but he was too hungry to go without dinner. It made him mad that every time they started in a new place, people treated them like bums. Lila always said that being honest was the most important thing in the world. But what good did it do to be honest when everybody expected you to lie and steal? Grady wanted to run off with Charlie Fernwald's truck and leave it in a junkyard a hundred miles away. He could do it, too. He had learned to drive a tractor on their first commune when he was seven and had been driving anything he could get his hands on ever since.

If he did steal the truck, Grady knew he would be

getting Lila into trouble as much as himself. He'd have to be satisfied with just picturing old Charlie red faced and sputtering. Grady wished he could really do it, though. It would serve Charlie right for not trusting them.

CHAPTER
6

Grady could tell that his mother was spending most of the twenty dollars on stuff she wanted to cook for Charlie. "Hey, that was supposed to be for our food. Besides, the old coot doesn't even want you to cook for him."

Lila examined nine zucchinis before she found the three she wanted and put them in her basket. "That's what he thinks now, but I'm going to turn his thinking clear around. You just wait and see."

"Well, you're not going to turn him around with zucchini squashes, that's for sure." Right away Grady wished he hadn't said that. Why couldn't he just keep his mouth shut and let her have her little dreams? It didn't take much to make Lila happy.

Grady left his mother sorting through the carrots

and wandered around the store until he came to the toy aisle. It was the usual junk—crummy plastic stuff sealed to little cards with more plastic. He used to beg for toys like these when he was younger, thinking each one was a little treasure just waiting for him to open it. Funny how you see things different when you grow up. The only thing that looked even halfway interesting to him now was a plastic slingshot, but he could tell it would probably break on the first try. He held it up, card and all, and pretended to be taking aim at one of the ceiling lights. Right away a pimply-faced kid wearing a big red Hokey Pokey Grocery pin stopped piling up boxes of diapers and came toward him.

"You gonna buy that? Because if you're not, you'd better put it down right now or else."

Grady tried to figure out how old he was. Sixteen, maybe seventeen at the most. "Or else what?"

The guy didn't have an answer for that.

"Look, Hokey," Grady said, "I don't want to buy this thing, but I might be interested in renting it. How much would it be to rent it overnight? Maybe two nights?"

The kid jutted out his chin. "Oh, a smart guy,

huh? Well, for your information, Hokey Pokey is the name of the store. And we don't do rentals."

"You ought to bring it up with the manager."

"I am the manager. Front end manager, four-thirty to midnight."

This guy had just handed Grady such a great straight line, he was tempted to go into a string of one-liners about what a rear end manager might do. But Grady figured this guy didn't have a sense of humor and there was nobody nearby to hear the jokes. No fun in that. Besides, Grady was so hungry his stomach had gone beyond growling and was moving up to barking. He put the slingshot back on its hook and went to find Lila.

She was checking out with a bunch of veggies and some baking stuff. "What's for dinner?" Grady asked.

Lila pulled two jars out of her cart. Peanut butter and jam. Not the good kinds, either. Hokey Pokey brand. And a loaf of bread that had *day old* scrawled across the wrapper in purple marker. Grady gave the loaf a squeeze. That *day old* must have been written on there a week ago.

Grady didn't try to hide his disappointment. It

wasn't fair. That money was supposed to be for their food, not Charlie's. Lila reached over and rubbed Grady's back. "You and me can make do for a few days, Grady. Just till we're settled in for good."

Grady nodded. It wasn't the first time they'd had to "make do," and he'd eaten lots worse than stale peanut butter sandwiches. He wasn't going to bust Lila's bubble again.

One of the lights in the parking lot was broken, so Grady almost ran their cart into a guy who was standing by a car having a smoke. Lila had parked Charlie's truck under the other light, so it was easy to find, not that the lot was all that big. As Lila pulled out onto the road, Grady opened the lid of the peanut butter jar and scooped his finger into it. Not bad. It might be a cheapo brand, but at least it was chunky.

Lila glanced over. "Don't you be eating in this truck."

"Why not?"

"This here's practically a new truck, Grady. Can't be more'n four, maybe five years old. Still has a little new car smell to it. Least it did before you opened that jar."

Grady thought it smelled more like old Charlie

than new car. He was busy fishing for another finger-ful of peanut butter, so he didn't say anything.

Lila saw him in the light of a passing neon sign. "You in that jar again? Can't you wait till we get home?"

"Mom, I'm half starved!"

She sighed. "All right, but don't be getting none of that peanut grease on these seats or I'll give you what for when we get home. Charlie has trusted his truck with me, and it's going back in the same shape I took it out."

Lila was always threatening to give him "what for." One time Grady had asked her what "what for" was, and she said he didn't want to find out. So far he hadn't.

They were about halfway back to Charlie's when Lila put her hand on Grady's arm. The rearview mirror made a band of light across her eyes. "I don't want you to be scared or nothing, but I think somebody is following us. Can you see who it is?"

Grady closed the jar and turned around in his seat. "All I can see is headlights, Mom. Just keep going. We can't be that far from Charlie's."

"Did you see that weird guy in the parking lot?" Lila asked. "It's not him, is it? He was watching us all the way back to the truck."

Grady wanted to tell her that wasn't a big deal. Guys were always watching her on account of how pretty she was. But he didn't think that would calm her down any. "It's prob'ly nothing, Mom, but if it bothers you, speed up a little so we lose him."

Lila gave the truck some more gas and leaned close to the steering wheel, squinting at the road ahead. "I wish I knew these parts better. Hard to see where we are. Is he still coming after us, Grady? I don't dare look back."

Grady knelt on the seat backward. "He's right behind us."

Lila sped up some more, but so did the other car. Grady was beginning to think she was right. That guy really was following them. Probably thought a small woman and a skinny kid were fair game. But Grady knew his mother was a lot stronger than she looked and so was he. He felt around behind the seat to see if Charlie kept a tire iron there, but all he found was some spare change. All of a sudden he saw the big Fernwald Farm sign at the end of Charlie's driveway. "Hey, Mom! We missed it! We just passed Charlie's place!"

"You sure?"

"Yeah. I saw the sign."

"That guy still behind us?"

"Yep. Right on our tail."

"All right. I got to find a place to turn around. This road ain't wide enough for a U-turn. You keep your eyes peeled for a driveway."

All of a sudden the dashboard glowed red for a second, then again. Grady looked in the side mirror and saw flashing red lights behind them.

"Oh, jeez! Mom, you gotta stop!"

"I'm not stopping till I get us home safe."

"But Mom, it's a cop!"

"Just because someone has a flashing red light on his car don't make him no cop, Grady. They have catalogs where you can order flashing lights and sirens for your car and badges and everything. I just heard on the radio the other day about a man who fooled people into thinking he was a cop with that stuff. Then you know what he did? He murdered them."

The red lights were next to them now as the car passed them.

"They don't have Morgan County Sheriff cars in no catalog, Mom."

The sheriff's car had slowed ahead of them, blocking the road.

"I see your point, Grady," Lila said, and she pulled Charlie's truck over to the shoulder.

It took a long time for the sheriff to come back to their car. Lila had pulled about fifty things out of her purse before she found her driver's license, but she had it ready and the window rolled down by the time he got to them.

"I'm sorry, Officer. Was I goin' over the speed limit? I thought you were some weirdo pursuing me and my offspring, Grady, here. I'm not familiarized with these roads on account of I'm new to these parts."

"You may be new around here," the sheriff said, "but this truck isn't."

"That's exactly right," Lila said, giving the sheriff a big smile. "This here truck belongs to Mr. Charlie Fernwald, for which I've been hired to be a personal dietitian. I was in town getting the food for his meals tomorrow and I missed seeing his driveway back there."

The sheriff touched the wide brim of his hat. "I thought that might be your problem. There's a farm with a circle driveway up ahead. Follow me and I'll flash the red lights again when we approach Charlie's driveway."

"That's real nice of you, Officer. Thanks."

Lila followed the sheriff's car down the road to the turnaround. "Isn't he the sweetest thing? Can you imagine he knew Charlie's truck? Must be a real friendly town if everybody knows each other that well. We were lucky he happened to come along."

"He didn't just happen to come along, Mom. Charlie said he was going to call the sheriff to check up on us. He was afraid we'd run off with his truck."

"Why, I would never do such a thing."

"Yeah, well, tell that to your old friend Charlie and see how far it gets you."

The red lights were flashing now. The sheriff stopped a little past Charlie's driveway and waited until they turned, in case they were really trying to steal Charlie's stupid old truck, Grady figured.

Lila drove slowly down the driveway. "Well, at least we got home safe."

As they neared the house, Grady saw Charlie pull back the curtains to watch them. "Yeah," Grady said. "Nothing like home, sweet trusting home."

CHAPTER
7

Lila dropped Grady off at the cottage so he could make the sandwiches while she returned the truck and keys. By the time she got back, he had already polished one off, along with three good-sized fingers of peanut butter on the side. He washed another sandwich down with a glass of milk, then made up his cot in the closet and went to bed. Sleeping in a closet wasn't as bad as it sounded. He could even read by the light of the ceiling bulb if he wanted to. Grady liked the privacy but was glad there was a curtain instead of a real door. At least he wouldn't die in his sleep from lack of air.

And he liked having a spot to call his own, even if it was a room barely big enough to hold his bed. In their first commune he slept in the boys' bunkhouse, and the places after that he always shared a small room with Lila. This was definitely a step up. Charlie Fernwald's farm was turning out to be a six or seven.

Grady must have been tired, because the next thing he knew, he woke in the morning to the smell of something baking. He stuck his head through the curtain door. "Is it pancakes?"

Lila looked up with a spot of flour on her nose. "It's zucchini carrot bread for Charlie."

Grady swung his knees out the door and went over to the table. The linoleum floor was cold on his bare feet. He pulled out the chair near the oven to warm up. Lila shoved the loaf of day-old store bread across the table. "Make yourself some toast. There's jam and peanut butter, if you want it."

"Oh, good, something different," Grady said. "I sure was getting sick of those peanut butter sandwiches."

"Don't give me none of your lip, Grady. I want you to take this up to Charlie soon as you've ate and got dressed."

"Aw, Mom. He's not going to eat any of your veggie stuff."

"Yes, he is, because this bread is as sweet as honey and nobody's going to tell him about those veggies

I hid inside, hear? Hurry up so he gets it while it's still hot."

After Grady had his peanut butter toast sandwich and slid back into his clothes, he headed up to the big house with Lila's bread. She had wrapped it in a few layers of paper towels, but it warmed his fingers as he trudged through the cold.

Charlie was out in the yard, working on one of his antennas. He had lowered the part with the spokes so they were only about chest high and was fastening some big white gourds to the end of each one with wire. Charlie looked over his shoulder when he heard Grady come up behind him. "You need something?"

"No. My mom sent this up for you."

"What's that?"

"Bread. Homemade. It's still hot."

Charlie went back to fastening the gourds to the antenna. "I told your mother she didn't need to cook for me. Take it back and tell her thanks, but no thanks."

"I'm not telling her that. She's going to keep on cooking for you, so you might as well eat it."

Charlie took the bread from Grady, lifted a corner of the paper towel, and sniffed. "What's in it?"

"Nothing that's going to jump out and bite you. It's baking stuff. Butter and sugar and flour, I guess."

Charlie raised his bushy eyebrows. "You sure? I thought your mother was one of those health food nuts."

Grady reached for the bread. Nobody was going to call his mother a nut. "Forget it. I'll eat it. The only food she bought for us was stale bread and lousy peanut butter. The rest was all for you."

"I told you I didn't want her to do that. The money was for your food, not mine."

"Well, she went ahead and done it and she's going to kill me if I bring it home, so I'm going to start eating it right now if you aren't."

Charlie kept a grip on the bread. "Now, don't be so hasty. I could use a break about now. How about we both go in and have a piece of this? Then maybe you could do me a favor by giving me some help with my gourds."

"The way you talk, you're doing me a favor by eating Mom's bread and I return the favor by working for you. Doesn't seem like an even trade to me."

Charlie shrugged and handed back the bread. "I thought you'd like to learn something new. It's all the same to me one way or the other."

Grady took the bread and stormed off toward the barn. He figured he could hunker down out of sight and enjoy his feast. Then he thought of something and ran back to Charlie. "Don't tell my mom I ate this, okay? If she asks, tell her you ate it and you liked it."

Charlie shook his head. "No, I can't do that. I won't tell a lie for anybody. Never did. Never will."

"It's no big deal," Grady said. "It's only a loaf of bread."

"It was a big deal to your mother or she wouldn't have gone to all the trouble of baking it."

Why was he trying to talk some sense into this old coot? Charlie was never going to go along with Lila's plans for him anyway. They should pack up their stuff right now and hitchhike out of town.

Charlie put down the gourd and started walking toward the house. He stopped on the porch steps and turned around. "Are you going to bring that bread or not?"

Now Grady was supposed to be a mind reader? "Yeah, I'm coming."

By the time Grady got to the house, Charlie was putting out two plates. He went to the refrigerator. "You need butter on this bread?"

"Not really. It's sort of like cake."

Charlie's head was in the refrigerator. "You should have told me that in the first place. I never met a cake I didn't like." He opened a carton of milk and smelled it, then held it out. "You think this has gone bad?"

Grady could tell from across the room that it had. The whole refrigerator smelled like it had gone bad. He nodded.

Charlie poured it down the sink. "All I have is coffee. Black. You want that?"

"I don't care." Grady wasn't wild about coffee and Lila had a fit when he drank it, but at least it might warm him up.

"Have a seat, then." Charlie poured two mugs of coffee that looked like used motor oil, then cut the bread, sliding a plate with one piece across the table.

Grady took a sip of coffee. It made him shiver. It was bitter as sucking on a piece of raw rhubarb.

Charlie sat across from him and studied his slice of bread. Grady was hoping he wouldn't notice the little green and orange specks from the zucchini and carrots. He didn't. He broke off a piece and ate it. "Good. It is more like cake than bread. Nice and moist." He polished it off and took more.

They ate in silence. Grady had to take a bite of the

sweet bread after each sip of Charlie's mud coffee, but it did heat up his insides some.

"So . . . are you willing to help me out around here or not?"

"It's my mom you hired. I wasn't in the deal," Grady said.

"No, you weren't. But maybe we can work out our own deal."

Grady bent his head down so his hair fell over his eyes. That way he could watch Charlie without him knowing it. Whenever anybody started talking about making a deal, Grady put his radar into high gear. Lila had been cheated too many times, so it was his job to protect them.

"Every now and then there's a chore around here I could use some help with," Charlie said. "I'd pay by the job, not by the hour. That way you wouldn't be tempted to work slow to make more money."

"You got no right to call me lazy," Grady said. "I'm a hard worker."

Charlie nodded. "Fair enough. We'll figure out the pay for each job, one at a time. You interested?"

"Maybe." Grady shrugged. "Depends on the job . . . and the pay."

Charlie had been watching something out of the

big picture window. All of a sudden he jumped up and grabbed a pair of binoculars, twirling the little knob until he brought something into focus. "Dang! They're back already. I had a feeling they might be early!"

Grady looked out in the driveway but didn't see anything.

Charlie gulped the last of his coffee and grabbed his jacket. "Come on! I'll introduce you."

Grady followed him out on the porch. "Hey, Marie!" Charlie shouted. "Welcome home!"

He was running out to the antennas, looking up, but there was nothing in sight. All of a sudden Grady figured it out. There had been a man at their first commune—Spaceman, they called him—who was always seeing UFOs. He claimed he could bring aliens in for a landing by flapping bedsheets at them. Grady was only a little kid then, and Spaceman had him convinced that a flying saucer with little green men was going to land right in the middle of that commune. Grady practically wore his eyes bloodshot staring at the sky, but never saw a single thing.

Spaceman told Grady he couldn't see the UFOs because he didn't believe in them hard enough. He said if Grady stood out under the stars all night balanced on one leg, those aliens would see he was sincere and they'd make themselves visible to him. Grady tried. Lord, how he tried. But he couldn't keep his balance for more than a few minutes at a time. After about an hour, Spaceman showed up with a bunch of other guys and shone a flashlight on Grady on one leg with his arms pinwheeling to keep balanced. Everybody had laughed. What a rotten trick to play on a little kid.

Grady never did find out if Spaceman really believed in aliens or if he was just playing a joke, because after Lila heard about what had happened she packed up and they left the next morning. "Ain't nobody going to treat my boy like that," she had said.

That's when Grady learned that you had to watch out for people. "Don't trust nobody right off until you get to know 'em," Lila had told him. "And even then, you got to keep an eye on 'em. There's good people in this world and there's bad people, but ain't no tellin' which is which by their looks." Grady had remembered that advice and followed it. Unfortunately, Lila's trusting nature often made her forget her own wise words.

Grady watched old Charlie Fernwald dancing

around the yard under the poles, waving his arms and calling out to his imaginary friends in the sky. So that's what the weird antennas were for. Charlie was trying to lure in aliens with his contraptions. No wonder Roger wanted somebody to baby-sit his father. Charlie Fernwald was crazy as a stinkbug on a hot sidewalk.

CHAPTER

8

Grady tried to slip past Charlie and go back to the cottage, but he wasn't fast enough. "Hey, don't run off when I have a job for you, boy. Give me a hand here."

A job? Grady didn't want to get roped into Charlie's fantasy world. On the other hand, if there was some money involved, he'd be a fool to pass it up. What could it hurt, anyway? He could humor the old guy and end up with some spare change in his pocket.

Charlie must have read his mind. "Twenty-five cents for each gourd you fasten to the rack. Deal?"

Grady did some fast mental math. There were three poles with eight spokes on each one. Charlie had put six gourds on the first pole. So that left eight times two—sixteen, plus two—eighteen, divided by four— four dollars and fifty cents.

"You just going to stand there, or do we have a deal?"

"Deal."

It wasn't hard work. Each gourd had a thick plastic-covered wire threaded through two holes in the top. Charlie showed Grady how to wind each end of the wire along the spoke. "Leave a little play in it so the gourd can swing some. They like that."

"Oh, I bet they do," Grady said. "Must be like a little carnival ride for 'em." Figured he might as well play along. Charlie gave him a funny look but didn't say anything. Grady had three gourds fastened up in no time. One more and he'd have a dollar. "What are those funny-shaped holes in the front for?" Grady asked.

"Each gourd has an entrance hole for them to get inside," Charlie said. "It's shaped like a crescent to keep their enemies from getting in."

"What about the Batman-shaped holes?" Grady was picturing little green aliens in tights and capes.

"Same thing," Charlie said. "They're new. I'm trying them out to see which ones work best. Then I'll send in a report at the end of the season."

Grady grinned. "To galaxy headquarters?"

"What's that you say?"

Grady didn't want to get Charlie upset before he

was paid. "Nothing. I'm counting my quarters." Man! This guy thought he had space wars going on in his own backyard. "So what does the enemy look like?" Grady asked, egging Charlie on.

"I've got pictures in the house," Charlie said. "I'll show you later."

Pictures, huh? This was going to be fun. In spite of the fact that he knew it was crazy, Grady felt himself being drawn back into the old excitement of seeing little green men from outer space. After all, it was a big universe. Nobody had ever proved that they *didn't* exist. And Grady was too old and too smart to get tricked by Charlie if he was playing a joke.

Charlie picked up his binoculars again. "They show up, then take right off. Trying to make me think they're not going to stay here. They'll be back, though. They always come back. You ever seen them?"

Should he admit to his UFO experience? Sure, why not? It would be interesting to see what Charlie would say. "Almost. I mean I knew someone who could see them, but I didn't."

"What in tarnation are you talking about, boy? Either you've seen martins or you haven't."

Martins? That was funny. Charlie couldn't even pronounce *martians* right. Old Charlie Fernwald wasn't as smart as he pretended to be. That made Grady feel better—less vulnerable. He went over to the pile of gourds and grabbed a couple more. An easy fifty cents.

Charlie had finished loading the second pole and came over to help Grady with the last one. "Poor things have had a long trip. They spend their winters in Brazil. And they come back to the same house every year. Sure is a big day when they come back. There's not a sight in the world prettier than a flock of purple martins."

"Purple? I thought they were green."

"Being smart now, are you?" Charlie shook his head. "After my wife died, I thought my life was over, then Roger got me my first gourd rack. Most people around here have a hard time attracting martins. Not me. Four days after I put up the rack, in they came. I've been a purple martin landlord ever since."

All of a sudden a small dark shape tumbled out of the sky and skimmed so close to Grady's face, he could feel the breeze on his cheek.

"It's Marie!" Charlie yelled. "She's usually one of the first ones back. She's after you because you're holding her gourd. Better hurry. We still need to put the pine needles in."

The thing swooped at Grady again, and this time he swatted at it. Charlie caught his wrist. "What's the matter with you? I won't have you hurting my birds."

Birds? Grady looked up. There were five of them circling overhead, making a bright chattering sound. While Grady was standing there with his mouth open, Charlie fastened on the last of the gourds. Then he started unscrewing caps on the side of each gourd and stuffing pine needles inside. "Come on," he said, grabbing a handful of needles out of a bushel basket. "They're getting impatient. Put two or three inches of needles in each gourd."

"What for?" Grady asked.

"Nests," Charlie said. "We're making nests for them."

"Don't birds usually build their own nests?"

Charlie screwed the last cap back on and started cranking the gourds up the pole with a winch. "These aren't usual birds. Besides, they're tired. They've just flown in from Brazil, remember? I like to give them a soft bed to sleep on."

The birds were landing on the rack before it reached the top of the pole. Charlie raised up the last rack. "Here it comes, Marie. Gourd number twenty-one. Home, sweet home." Even before the gourds stopped moving, the bird Charlie called Marie folded her wings close to her body and dove into the entrance hole marked twenty-one.

Charlie's face was red, either from excitement or all the rushing around. "Isn't that a sight? Every year they find their way back to my farm."

There were more birds overhead now. "How do you know they're the same birds as last year? They all look alike to me."

"I can't tell most of them apart, but I know Marie. First off, she always claims the same gourd. And if you look closely, you'll see she's the only one with a band on her leg."

"Did you put that on her?"

"No, you have to be a licensed bander to do that. It was probably done at her first colony where she hatched and fledged. Probably someplace thirty to fifty miles from here."

"Then why did she come here? I thought you said they always go back to the same house."

"I've read that only about one out of ten martins return to their original colony the second year. I'm not sure why that is, but it's a good thing, because that's how new colonies get started. The second year martins are looking for a place to live, and from then on they stay loyal to their new colony. Anyway, Marie has always been my favorite. She's the best acrobat. Her antics will make you laugh right out loud."

Grady wasn't sure if he was disappointed or relieved that Charlie's visitors were only birds. Not that he had really believed in aliens, but after all the buildup, this was pretty tame. Maybe when you got to be an old geezer, you could get all worked up about bird watching, but it sure wasn't Grady's idea of a good time. Now he was wondering if Charlie would really pay up. He stood around for a few minutes, hoping Charlie would remember the money, but the old man was too involved with his birds to think about anything else. Grady stepped closer. "I guess I'm all through here now. I'd better go back and see if Mom needs anything."

Charlie was barely listening to him, keeping his eyes glued on those darn birds. "All right." He gave a halfhearted wave—a gesture of dismissal. Grady waited to see that hand reach for his wallet. Nothing.

Grady cleared his throat. "I mean unless you have another *job* for me to do."

That remark brought Charlie out of his bird trance. "Oh, right, I owe you some money here. How many gourds did you do?"

"Six, I think. Maybe seven." Grady wished he had

been faster. All that time he'd wasted staring, he could have been earning more quarters. Next time he'd be smarter.

Charlie pulled out two dollar bills.

"I don't have change," Grady said.

Charlie smiled. "So you'll owe me a quarter. Thanks for the help."

Before Grady could answer, Charlie was talking to his birds again.

Well, he wasn't another UFO nut, but believing these birds flew back and forth to Brazil every year was as crazy as thinking aliens were landing in the yard. The old guy was probably harmless, though, and for the first time in his life, Grady had a little spending money of his own.

CHAPTER
9

Lila was pleased pink that Charlie had liked her bread. "Didn't I tell you, Grady? There's no way he could resist my bread fresh from the oven like that. Why, that aroma grabs your taste buds in a stranglehold."

"Kinda hard to swallow that way, isn't it?" Grady asked.

Lila gave him a gentle punch on the arm. "Never mind, smart mouth. You know I'm a good cook. And tonight I'm going to make Charlie Fernwald the best dinner he ever ate."

"Don't push your luck, Mom. Maybe he liked the bread, but that doesn't mean he's going to let you cook him dinner."

Lila stood at the open refrigerator door, studying

its contents. "Leave me be, Grady. I'm figuring out a menu."

"Well, whatever you make, you better freeze it in a little cardboard box he can heat up in his microwave, or he's not going to eat it. That man is real set in his ways."

A sudden knock on the door made them both jump. Lila peeked out the window. "It's him," she whispered. "Don't you say nothing to upset him."

Grady sighed. "He probably wants me to help with his birds again."

Lila smoothed back her hair and opened the door. "Well, isn't this a nice surprise. You just come right on in here, Mr. Fernwald, and make yourself to home." She gestured toward the only comfortable chair in the room.

Charlie stood in the doorway. He was so tall, the house seemed built for elves. Funny, he wasn't stooped over like most of the old geezers Grady had seen. "No need for me to come in. I wondered if you could do me a favor."

Grady shot him a sideways glance. Here it comes, Grady thought. He's got something else for me to do, but if he calls it a favor, there won't be any pay. Grady moved to the far corner of the room—an empty gesture because it was only three steps away.

"I'd surely be pleased to do you a favor," Lila said, her face all bright and smiley. "You tell me what it is, and it's as good as done."

"Well, I was wondering . . ." Charlie had taken off his John Deere cap and was working his fingers around the brim. "My son and his wife have invited themselves over tomorrow. They're coming around one o'clock."

"I suspect they want to see how good a cook I am. I think we should give them a fine Sunday dinner, don't you?"

Charlie smiled and nodded. He seemed relieved not to have to say it himself. "Just because it's Sunday dinner doesn't mean you have to go all out, though. Anything will be fine. And this doesn't mean I want you to start cooking for me. It's a onetime favor."

Lila raised her eyebrows and sent a smug look across the room to Grady. "Now, that's no favor at all. It's what I was hired for in the first place."

"Oh, and one more thing," Charlie said. "Could you make sure you cook a vegetable? Roger's wife, Ethel, is still fussing about me staying here alone. If she sees me eating vegetables, that should win her over. Try to make it something that tastes halfway decent, though. Nothing green."

"Well, vegetables just happen to be my specialty. I can make an acorn squash taste better than a hot fudge sundae."

Grady tried not to smile. He knew that statement was a big exaggeration.

Charlie seemed dubious, too. "Pretty sure of yourself, aren't you?"

"I don't mean to sound prideful, Mr. Fernwald. I'm only speaking the honest truth."

"I guess I'll be the judge of that." Charlie reached in his pocket and handed Lila some money. "I suppose you'll need to get extra food in. Will this cover it?"

"It surely will, because I pride myself on being good at spotting a bargain. Not that I ever skimp on quality, but I can make a dollar go farther than anybody you ever met."

Grady's sigh made Charlie notice him for the first time. "Have you been watching my birds, Grady? You can see them from your front window, can't you?"

"You didn't say I had to watch them."

"Tarnation, you don't *have* to watch them. I thought you'd *like* to. They're pretty interesting. Better than watching TV."

"We don't *have* a TV," Grady said. He was still annoyed about that.

Charlie put his cap back on his head. "Then I guess you're lucky to have the martins to keep you entertained." Charlie closed the door before Grady could think of a comeback. He wasn't about to watch any stupid birds. Not unless he got paid good money to do it.

When Lila went off to buy the food, Grady stayed in the cottage. He made up his cot in the closet, smoothing out the bedspread. Then he propped up his pillows and stretched out. A long horizontal board against the back wall made a narrow shelf just about eye level when he was sitting up. Grady hung over the edge of the bed and pulled out his backpack. He could put his stuff on that shelf, make things more homelike. He lined up his toothbrush, a small plastic comb, his book, and the red Corvette Matchbox car his dad had given him the last Christmas he was alive.

Grady's dad was always on the lookout for an old Corvette he could fix up, but he never had found one he could afford, except for one that was smashed beyond repair. Grady had known there was something special in that tiny package on that last Christmas morning. He could tell by the way his father watched him open it. "Someday," his dad said, "I'll find us a real Corvette, Grady. And you and me will fix it up so it runs good as new. Then we'll paint it candy apple red, just like this one."

Now, as he ran that little car across the shelf, Grady's eyes stung with the tears he never showed to anybody. He could picture his father at the wheel, laughing. What a time they would have had in that car. How different their lives would have been if it hadn't been for the accident. Grady shook his head and pushed the memories aside. Feeling sorry for himself only made things worse. He parallel parked the Corvette between the comb and the toothbrush, then leaned back on his pillows and looked at his tiny room. It wasn't bad, now that he had his stuff out where he could see it. It felt more like home than anywhere he'd been in a long time. This place could be a seven and a half or an eight.

The next day, Grady helped Lila lug the groceries up to the kitchen in the big house. "I'm going to need about forty-five minutes to myself, Grady. Your job is to keep that man out of his kitchen while I'm trying to cook."

"How am I supposed to do that?"

"I don't know. Ask him about those birds of his. That'll keep him going for a while. I don't want him coming in here snooping around."

Grady went into the living room. Charlie was sitting at the table with a pen in his hand and a notebook in front of him, looking out the window at his birds. He glanced up when Grady came into the room. "Have a seat. They're all flying around the gourds now. Putting on a good show. Look how they swoop around on those graceful wings of theirs."

Grady plopped into the chair opposite Charlie. There were a couple dozen birds now from what Grady could see. "More of 'em came, huh?" Good. Question number one. That wasn't hard. Only about forty-four more bird questions ought to fill the time until dinner.

Charlie took the bait for question number one.

"This is only half of what we'll get if it's a good year. We've got housing up for forty-eight."

Grady noticed Charlie was talking in terms of "we," as if the birds were partly his. "Oh, so you get two birds to each house?"

"Well, sure. You need a pair. A male and a female."

Rats! That was a stupid question and it didn't take up much time. Grady's mind was racing to find a third question but he didn't need to. Charlie was off and running. He pushed the notebook across the table. "This gives all the numbers from last year and the dates they arrived. They're right on schedule. I've been watching their progress on the Internet, too. The first wave is about ready to cross over Lake Erie to Canada."

"They show that on the Internet?"

"Yep. The first reports always come from Florida— Naples and Marco Island in late December or early January. Then by late January they're showing up in Texas—Corpus Christi and San Antonio. Seems like it's easier to get martins down South. They say you hang up an old boot in Texas and the martins will move right in. Up here there aren't nearly as many martins, so it's more of a challenge. Some people try for years and never get them. Come on, I'll show you the scout report map."

Grady followed Charlie into a small room with a computer on a desk. Funny, he didn't think of an old guy like Charlie having a computer. "You got any games on this?" he asked.

"Don't have time for games," Charlie said. "I use it for e-mail and the purple martin forum. And researching anything else I need to know."

Grady looked around the room. All four walls were filled with bookshelves. He'd never seen so many books in somebody's house before. "Wow! This is like a library."

Charlie sat down and turned on the computer. "I guess it is. We never had much of a library in town, so I started buying my own books years ago. Picked up a lot of these at secondhand book stores when I used to travel some."

"Where is the library in town?" Grady asked.

"There isn't one now. They combined with the big one over in Addieville. That's almost fifteen miles away. Seems a shame folks have to go so far to get a book."

Grady's heart fell. He was hoping he'd be able to

walk to a library. He wouldn't have minded walking to town from here to get a book. But fifteen miles, that was another thing altogether.

There hadn't been a library in the nearest town to Sunward Path, and the school at the commune was a joke. They were supposed to have class every day, but Rayden was the official teacher and he was more interested in himself than the kids, only holding one or two classes a week and then mostly rambling on with his "philosophizing," as Lila called it. Or sometimes he'd have the kids make stuff for the commune to sell. The last project was candle making. Since handling melted wax was too dangerous for the younger kids, Grady did most of the work. That took up three whole "school" days, and Rayden kept all the profits from selling the candles.

Charlie got up and pulled a book off the shelf. "Here's a good bird guide. It has a whole section on swallows. That's what purple martins are, you know. We have them all here—barn swallows, cliff swallows, and tree swallows." Charlie was flipping through the pages, pointing to different birds. They all looked the same to Grady. You've seen one bird, you've seen 'em all.

"These are the ones you have to watch out for," Charlie was saying, "the tree swallows. If you let a pair nest in your martin housing, they'll chase off all your martins. That's what that gourd on the short pole is for. I have a pair of tree swallows nesting in that now. They're so territorial, they'll chase off all the other tree swallows, so now it's clear sailing for the martins."

Grady looked out at the lower gourd. Sure enough, there was a dark blue and white head sticking out of the entrance hole. "How did you make the tree swallows go into the right house?" This was a real question—not that he was interested in birds. Just curious.

Charlie was back at the computer. "It's all on the Internet. The PMCA—Purple Martin Conservation Association—has a Web site with a message board. You got a question, somebody will have the answer. Look, here's the Scout Arrival study or, as some of us purple martin landlords call it, the 'Purple Wave.' Pull up that other chair."

There was a map of the United States on the screen that looked like somebody had spilled grape syrup on it. A wavy line spread north from the Gulf of Mexico. "Here's where we are," Charlie said, pointing at the screen near the top edge of the grape spill. "The best time is when the wave is almost up to where you live. It's like waiting for Christmas."

Grady wasn't sure what to think. If it was only Charlie going on about his birds, Grady could dismiss him as being a nut. But there must be lots of people wild about purple martins if they had a whole Web site and a real organization. Grady leaned in to get a better look. "Where are we, anyway?"

"I showed you. The town is called Bedelia."

"Yeah, I know that, but what state are we in?"

Charlie glanced over his shoulder. "I'd say you're in a state of confusion. This is Pennsylvania. Don't they teach geography in the schools anymore?"

"Well, we've moved around a lot, so I don't always get a whole year in one school. And we didn't learn nothing in the commune school."

"Commune!" Charlie spun his chair all the way around to face him. "Tarnation! They still have hippies? I thought they went out in the sixties."

Grady could feel his face getting hot. "We're not hippies. I told you, we move a lot, is all. And I'm not dumb. Once I read about something, I don't forget it."

"Well, then we'd better get you some reading material. Here, start with this atlas of the United States. And here's a bird book. What else are you interested in?"

Grady looked around at the shelves. There were lots of things that interested him—a book about wolves, another about airplanes, and the Chilton's auto mechanic's manual like the one his father had owned. He pulled that one off the shelf.

"You interested in fixing cars, are you?"

"Maybe," Grady said.

"You could start on an old tractor. That's what I did when I was your age. I have one back of the barn you could work on with me. I want to get it running good enough to sell."

"You're a mechanic?" Grady asked, trying to picture Charlie under a car.

"Every farmer's a mechanic. You have to be. When your tractor goes down in the middle of planting, you can't wait for somebody to come fix it." Charlie pulled another book from the shelf and rubbed the dust off the spine. "Here's some other books you might like. This section by the window has some books I got for my grandson when he was a kid. Fiction, mostly. That's the only part that's organized. You can borrow anything you want, long as you take care of it and bring it back when you're finished. Understand?"

Grady couldn't imagine anybody owning so many books. This was like having his own library. If he ever had a house someday, he was going to line the walls with books exactly like this.

"Guess I'll go in and see how your mother is doing with the meal," Charlie said.

Grady was so intent on looking at the books, Charlie was out of the room before he realized what was happening. He came to his senses in time to head Charlie off right before the kitchen. "I'll go see if Mom needs help. That's supposed to be my job. I'm her assistant."

"Well, I was only going to take a peek. Something smells pretty good."

Grady blocked the kitchen door. "Yeah, well, Mom doesn't like to have people watching her when she cooks."

"Oh, an artiste, is she?"

"Something like that."

"All right. I don't want to cramp her style." Charlie went back to the table with his bird notebook. "Remind her that Roger and Ethel will be here at one. They're always prompt. Sometimes early. I think Ethel wants to catch me doing something senile so she can put me in a home."

Charlie grinned, so Grady realized he was joking. Grady grinned back at him. "Okay, I'll tell her."

When Grady got into the kitchen, he could see why Lila didn't want Charlie in there. She was sneaking vegetables into everything—green vegetables.

"Aw, Mom, what are you doin' that for? Can't you cook something normal?"

"Grady, I may only have one chance to get some vitamins into that man, and I'm going to squeeze in as many as possible."

"But brussels sprouts? He's gonna taste them for sure. You want him to throw up in front of his son? That'll get you fired."

"Don't you worry your head about that. I can hide anything in a nice seasoned sauce." Lila shoved the brussels sprouts and some spinach into the blender and spun them into a green mush. Then she poured the stuff into a pot.

"Oh, yeah. He's goin' to love that. Smells like something that came out the back of a lawn mower."

"You get out of here and let me work. And keep that man busy, hear?"

"Yeah, I hear."

Twenty-four hours ago, Grady wouldn't have cared if Lila got fired. They could move on to another place, maybe better, maybe worse. But now he wasn't sure he wanted to go. If he could have all those books to read . . . if he could work on repairing a tractor . . . well, there was no sense getting worked up over it. He had learned long ago that it didn't pay to get attached to things or people, because he couldn't count on anything to stay the way it was for long. As Lila always said, "Enjoy what you have when you have it. Not one single thing in this world lasts forever."

CHAPTER
10

To Grady's amazement, Charlie never did notice the vegetables that Lila had hidden in the food that day. In fact, nobody did. They all thought the dinner was delicious. Roger made an announcement over dessert. "Ethel and I are so grateful that you came our way, Lila. Now we can head off for Florida knowing that my father is in good hands."

"I don't need to be in anybody's hands, Roger," Charlie said. "I was doing just fine with my TV dinners." But then he mopped up every last bit of sauce with his bread, leaving his plate so clean you could have put it right back in the cupboard without washing it. Roger noticed that and winked at Lila. She couldn't help showing the pleasure she felt about winning Charlie over, and Grady couldn't miss the "I told you so" signals she was sending his way. Grady figured she deserved to gloat.

After Roger and Ethel left, Grady was helping his mother clean up. Charlie came into the kitchen. "You sure made an impression on Roger. Thanks for getting him off my back."

"I'm glad he liked the dinner," Lila said, scrubbing a pan. "Glad you liked it, too."

Charlie looked down, running his thumb back and forth along the edge of the counter. "Well, it made a nice change from my Salisbury steak TV dinners. I wouldn't mind having a little variety like that once in a while, maybe a couple times a week."

Lila shot a big grin over to Grady, but Charlie couldn't see it because her back was to him. "I'd be happy to cook meals for you whenever you like, Mr. Fernwald. You decide what you want and when you want it."

———————

On Tuesday, Charlie was back at the cottage asking Lila to cook dinner that night. He did the same thing a couple of days later. Grady was surprised that Lila didn't get pushy about cooking every day for Charlie.

When he commented on that to his mother, Lila said, "I'm biding my time, Grady, reeling him in nice and easy. Some things—and people—just can't be rushed."

Grady was helping Lila clean up in the big kitchen Thursday night when Charlie came in. "That was a fine meal, Lila."

Lila ducked her head modestly. "I'm pleased that you liked it, Mr. Fernwald. I'm happy to do it as often as you'd like. Cooking gives me joy."

Charlie nodded. "Well, now that I think about it, I've been in kind of a rut with those Salisbury steaks. I might like to have you cook dinner pretty often . . . well, maybe every night. You should choose the menu, though. Whatever you like to cook. And I wouldn't mind having leftovers for lunch once in a while—I mean, if you were going to throw something out. No sense in wasting good food."

Grady could see Lila fighting against the smile that made her lips twitch in the corners. "I'd be happy to cook lunch and dinner, Mr. Fernwald. I make a mighty good breakfast, too, if you're interested."

"No, I'm pretty set in my ways about breakfast. Sugar Loops does me just fine, and I'm not much for company first thing in the morning. Just like to eat my cereal in peace and not have to say a word until I finish my second cup of coffee. You and your boy might as well eat your meals up here with me. Seems easier than lugging your food back to the cottage."

Lila rinsed the pot and set it in the drainer, then turned to face him. "Grady and me would be pleased to join you for meals."

"Fine, then, that's what we'll do." Charlie turned to Grady. "You still interested in working on that old tractor with me?"

"Sure."

"Okay, come on up to the barn tomorrow morning. I'll go out there right after I finish breakfast."

⊹⊹⊹⊹⊹

Grady was up Friday morning at dawn, watching for Charlie to come out of the house. He made himself hang around in the cottage for a few minutes so he wouldn't seem too anxious, then couldn't keep himself from running all the way to the barn.

"Let's start out with a little test so I can see how much you know," Charlie said.

The word *test* sent a chill up the back of Grady's neck, but he soon relaxed. Charlie showed him different tools and asked Grady if he knew what they were called and what they were used for. Charlie did a lot of talking, but this was interesting stuff, and Grady couldn't believe how fast the morning went by.

For the first few days, Grady was mostly fetching tools and holding things while Charlie explained how the engine worked. But by Friday of the next week, Charlie let him do some of the work.

"You pick things up real fast, Grady," Charlie said. "You seem to have a knack for engines."

Grady almost told Charlie right then about his father being a mechanic but decided he wasn't quite ready to trust him yet. He was pleased at the compliment, though, and just smiled to acknowledge it.

"My son, Roger, never took to fixing engines," Charlie went on. "Never took to farming, either. I had hoped the place would stay in the family, but none of the kids wanted it."

"You got other kids living around here?" Grady asked. He was trying to picture Charlie when he was younger with kids running around the farm.

"I have two daughters. They both met their husbands in college and moved away. Just about broke Marie's heart. She was real close to the girls. But they had their own lives. Can't hold your kids back. Can't let them hold you back, either, or push you around. Like selling this farm, for instance. I'll go when I'm ready to go, and that'll likely be feet first."

Grady was just thinking about what that "feet first" remark meant when there was a sudden loud chattering noise overhead and dozens of black birds descended on a tree behind the barn. "Blasted starlings," Charlie muttered. He went inside the barn and came out with a gun.

Grady moved warily behind the tractor. "You gonna shoot them birds?"

Charlie was loading the gun. "Wish I could get them all with one shot. The best I can do is shoot one and scare the tail feathers off the rest." He steadied the hand holding the gun barrel on the tire of the tractor while he took aim, then squeezed off a shot. Sure enough, one bird fell to the ground while the others scattered.

Grady heard footsteps racing down the driveway. It was Lila. "Grady! What happened? Are you all right?"

"He's fine," Charlie said. "I was just shooting at these dang starlings."

"But why?" Lila asked. "Why would you shoot at

some poor defenseless birds? It's one thing to kill for food, but doing it just for fun, well, that ain't right."

"Believe me, I don't do this for fun. If I can't keep these starlings away, they'll go after my martins. I shoot house sparrows, too. They're just as bad. Maybe worse. I can keep the starlings out of the gourds by using special entrance holes, but there's nothing that will keep house sparrows out if they want to get in and build a nest."

"I don't get it," Grady said. "You have so many gourds. Isn't there room for all of them?"

"You didn't read that bird book I lent you, did you, boy?"

Grady was going to make an excuse but thought better of it. He just shrugged.

"Well, if you had read it, you'd know that the starling and house sparrow are killers. Back in the 1800s, house sparrows were brought into this country to control an insect problem. They were adaptable and aggressive toward native songbirds, so they spread all over the country, wiping out many of our native cavity-nesting birds by taking over their nests, poking holes in eggs, and killing the young. That's what made bluebirds so scarce. And woodpeckers."

Lila shook her head. "That's hard to believe. Sparrows seem like such gentle creatures."

"I'm not talking about our native sparrows," Charlie said. "They never harm other birds. House sparrows are entirely different. They're an introduced species. That's why it's legal to trap and shoot them. And as if that weren't bad enough, some dang fool thought Central Park should have all of the birds mentioned in the works of Shakespeare, so he imported a whole bunch of birds from overseas and set them loose. They all died out except for the European starling. It was the same deal as the house sparrow. They were bullies and could adapt to any condition. They just took over, displacing and destroying native songbirds."

Here he goes again with another lecture, Grady thought. He had to admit that the martins were sort of interesting to watch, but why would you kill one kind of bird to save another? Didn't make any sense.

"Well, I don't care how bad those birds are," Lila said. "I don't want Grady anywhere near no guns."

"Don't worry. Nobody touches my gun but me. And I keep the ammunition where he can't get at it."

Lila started to say something else but sighed instead. "Well, all right. I got to go make dinner." She headed for the main house, but Grady saw her turn to check on them three times before she reached the door.

"Grady, give me a hand, will you? I need to get my trap out. Won't take long, and it's not heavy—just awkward for one person to handle."

This reminded Grady that there hadn't been any paid jobs for him since hanging the gourds. Charlie had made it clear that working on the tractor was a two-way thing because Grady was learning how to do engine repair while helping with the job. That seemed fair enough. Grady was eager to learn, and it was fun. The trap turned out to be nothing more than a big wire-and-wood cage with a V-shaped baffle at the top—not a big enough job to get paid for. "What can you catch with this?" Grady asked.

"Starlings or house sparrows. Both on a good day."

"Does this thing kill 'em?"

"No. I have to do that myself."

Charlie didn't say how, and Grady didn't want to know.

They carried the trap out under the big tree where the starlings had roosted earlier. Then Charlie went in and got some bread to toss inside the trap for bait.

When he came back to the tractor where Grady was waiting, he said, "Don't look at me that way, boy. Sometimes a person has to do things he doesn't like because they need doing. Someday you'll understand that."

Grady didn't think so, but he kept quiet. They worked side by side for a while.

Charlie kept getting distracted by the martins swooping overhead. He stopped to watch every time he heard them. "Just look at them up there. Doesn't it make you wish you could fly?"

Charlie dropped a small part when he looked up to see the birds fly over. "Grady, can you pick up that wing nut for me?"

"The what?"

"The wing nut I just dropped. It has two little projections on it that look like wings. It fell into that patch of grass."

Grady dropped to his knees and felt through the grass until he found it. He couldn't help smiling about the name—wing nut. That was the perfect description of Charlie Fernwald and his crazy attraction to birds.

For the next lesson, Charlie showed Grady how to replace a worn belt, then helped him get the right tension on it. When Grady finished, Charlie tugged on the belt and nodded his approval. "You're a bright boy. No reason why you can't make something of yourself." He straightened up and looked at Grady. "Come to think of it, you should be in school. You've been here two weeks, haven't you? Your mother needs to go into Addieville and get you registered."

Grady felt his stomach cramp up at the mention of school. "I don't go to regular school. I'm studying at home."

Charlie put down his wrench. "Really? You're doing that home-schooling business? I thought you said you went to some kind of school on that commune."

"That was only because Mom was so busy with the cooking and cleaning there. It took up all her time." Grady felt bad about lying to Charlie, but he was doing a lot of reading on his own, so that should count for something. And Charlie was the one who brought up the home schooling, not him.

"So your mother is teaching you now?" Charlie persisted. "I mean I've heard of home schooling, but each state is a little different, isn't it? Different regulations?"

Grady knew that once Charlie got on a subject, he was like a dog with a bone. Grady also knew he'd be digging himself in deeper if he tried to keep up with the home-schooling charade, because he didn't know a thing about it.

"You reminded me I'd better be getting back to work on my lessons right now. Mom will be checking up on me after dinner." As much as Grady hated to stop working on the tractor, he knew it was the only way to keep from giving himself away. If Charlie found out Grady was lying, he'd probably march him right off to school himself.

That night at dinner, Charlie was still gnawing on that home-schooling bone. "So Grady tells me you're teaching him, Lila. How does this home-schooling work, exactly?"

Grady jumped in before Lila could say anything. "Well, I do the work and Mom checks me on it, right, Mom?"

Lila caught his signal, so she didn't expose him, but Grady knew he'd have some big explaining to do later. "Grady's been doing a lot of reading. We're surely grateful to you for letting him borrow your books."

Charlie helped himself to another big piece of meat

loaf, which Grady knew was probably more broccoli than beef. "Reading my books is fine, and he's welcome to borrow any of them, but you do have some sort of plan, don't you?"

Lila looked puzzled. "Plan?"

"A lesson plan that you need to follow. Grady has to complete a certain amount of work for each grade, doesn't he? And does he take a test at the end of each year to make sure he's keeping up?"

Grady and his mother spoke at the same time.

"Sure, I take tests."

"There ain't no tests."

Charlie looked from one face to the other. "Which one of you is telling the truth here? Is this boy getting an education or isn't he?"

Grady stared at his plate. He couldn't think of what to say. He was a lousy liar in the first place and he could tell that Charlie saw right through his stupid story.

"He reads a lot, is all," Lila said in a small voice.

Charlie slapped the table. "Tarnation, Lila, you're the boy's mother. Are you going to let him grow up ignorant?"

Lila tilted her head and smiled weakly. Grady thought she looked like a kid who got caught with her finger in the peanut butter jar. "I been reading to that boy since he was a baby. And now that he's old enough to read himself, I make sure he gets his own library card every time we settle in a new town. Besides, I never had much learning myself and I manage all right. Nobody in our family ever had much schooling."

"That's no excuse," Charlie said. "Grady's got a quick mind. It's your responsibility to see he learns how to use it."

Lila spread her hands palm up on the table. "I don't know how to teach him. It's all I can do to make sure he's got food and a roof over his head. I'm doing the best I can. It's not easy raising a boy all by yourself."

"Well, maybe you should have thought of that before you went and got yourself in trouble," Charlie bellowed.

"But I've never been in no trouble, Charlie. Why, I always . . ." Then her face turned red as she realized what he was saying. "You mean you think . . . you think I . . ." She stood up. "Charlie Fernwald, you don't know the first thing about me."

"I know you'd be a lot better off now if you'd made sure you had a decent father for that boy. Young women nowadays think they can just have a baby with the first man who comes along and not give a thought to the future. Then the bum of a father runs off and you end up in a situation like this."

Lila's eyes were blazing mad. "I end up in a situation like this because my dear husband, Arlan Flood, the best man to ever walk the face of this earth, got himself killed while he was working hard to support me and his son. So don't you be on your high-and-mighty horse looking down your nose at us and thinking we're some sort of trash because there's no man in the family."

"Well, you never said anything about a husband, so I figured—"

"You figured wrong. And I didn't mention my husband because I been too busy trying to please you so I could keep this job." Lila took a step back, almost falling over her chair. "And don't you ever, EVER call Grady's father a bum again, because you're dead wrong."

Grady knew Charlie had stuck his foot in so deep, he might never get it out. It took a lot to get Lila mad, but saying anything bad about his father set her off worse than anything.

Lila stopped at the door and turned. "I don't feel

kindly toward you anymore, Charlie Fernwald, but I'm not gonna quit the job, because I need the money to save up for a car so we can get out of here." She took a deep breath. "But you can do your own dishes and clean up after yourself tonight. I just plumb ain't in the mood!"

CHAPTER
11

Grady saw Charlie's truck leave the driveway the next morning. He wondered if Charlie was mad at Lila for walking out without doing the dishes. He knew Lila was still furious at Charlie, because she was clearing the table from breakfast and slamming things a lot harder than she needed to as she took them to the sink.

Grady didn't blame Lila for being upset, but he could see why Charlie had misunderstood their situation. Half of the kids he'd met in their travels didn't have fathers living at home. He knew enough not to point that out to Lila while she was still fuming.

He went into the closet and flopped on his bed to get out of Lila's way. The old fears were nibbling at the edges of his mind again. What would happen if

Lila was mad enough to leave? Or what if Charlie fired Lila? How could they go anywhere without a car? He wasn't sure how much Lila was getting paid here. Was it enough for bus tickets? A bus to where? Lila took life as it came, but Grady knew they needed a plan. The problem was, he didn't have any idea what that plan ought to be.

When Grady started to read the latest book he had borrowed from Charlie's library, he couldn't keep his mind on the words. He reached for his copy of *Gilly Hopkins* instead. He let the book choose the page, opening itself to the part where Gilly was writing a letter to her mother. A familiar feeling of calm fell over him as he read. It was like visiting an old friend.

About an hour later, Grady heard Charlie's truck come back, followed shortly by a second truck. That was worth a trip to the window. Charlie hadn't had any visitors since Roger and Ethel left. This visitor was a big surprise. It was Sal Palvino towing a car on a hook behind his pickup. "What's he up to?" Grady said out loud. At first he thought it might be their old car, but when Sal's truck pulled past the cottage window, he could see that it was another junker.

"What's who up to?" Lila wiped her hands on a

dish towel and joined him at the window. "Isn't that the nice guy who went to look at our car and brought us out here?"

Grady shrugged. "I don't think so. Looks like some other guy." He went to sit on his bed, hoping Lila would go back to her work.

She did. "Well, I'm sure not interested in anything Mr. Charlie Fernwald might be doing," she said, clattering dishes in the sink with a vengeance.

Grady was dying to know what Charlie was going to do with that car. He yawned and stretched, trying to look bored. "I'm going to get me a breath of air."

Lila gave him a sharp look. "Since when are you so all-fired interested in air?"

Grady grinned. "I gotta breathe, don't I?"

"You can do all the breathing you want, but you stay away from Charlie Fernwald, hear?"

"We're going to see him for lunch, aren't we? How you gonna get around that?"

"I may have to cook for that man, but that don't mean we have to eat with him. I can bring our meal right back here." She plunged a pot into the sink so hard it made water slosh onto the floor.

Grady slipped outside and started toward the big

house. Sal was talking with Charlie. So much for him believing Grady about Charlie shooting trespassers. Charlie pointed toward the barn, then Sal moved the truck and unloaded the car where Charlie wanted it. Charlie saw Grady and motioned for him to come. Grady couldn't very well say no to his mother's boss. At least that's the argument he was going to use when Lila yelled at him later for talking to Charlie.

"Here's our new project, Grady," Charlie said, raising the hood. "Think we can get it back on the road?"

We? Grady looked at the engine. It was old and dirty, but there was no duct tape. "This yours?"

"It is now," Charlie said. "But I can sell it to your mother if she wants it. I paid Sal three hundred dollars for it. I'll sell it to her for the same amount. Won't even charge her the cost of parts to repair it, since you'll be doing part of the work. That sound fair?"

"I guess." The chance of Lila ever having three hundred dollars all at once was slim to none, but he didn't say so. Even though this engine looked different from the tractor engine, Grady could pick out the spark plugs, the carburetor, and the fan belt. Maybe he could learn enough so if they ever broke down at the side of the road again, he'd know what to do. Or better yet, he could stay on top of things so they wouldn't have any breakdowns in the first place. Grady leaned over the engine, breathing in the oily smell. It brought back the memory of his father's hands when he'd sneak up from behind and put them over Grady's eyes to play "guess who?"

Sal cranked the hook back up on his truck, then came over to shake hands with Charlie. "Let me know if you want anything. I can get parts for you cheap."

"Thanks," Charlie said. "Grady and I will look it over and see what we need. I'll give you a call."

Sal noticed Grady for the first time. "Hey, kid. How's it going? How's your mother?"

"Fine," Grady said, glaring. He wanted to say she had some terrible contagious disease that gives you bad breath and makes you fart every five minutes. What else would keep Sal away, now that he knew Charlie wouldn't shoot him?

Sal swung up into the cab of his truck and started the engine. "Well, say hello to her for me, kid." He slammed the door shut and started down the driveway.

"All right, Grady," Charlie said. "Let's go tell your mother about the car."

"Maybe this isn't the best time to talk to her," Grady said.

"She's still mad?"

"Oh, yeah," Grady said. "Big time."

Charlie took off his John Deere cap, pushed the fringe of hair behind his ears, and put the cap back on. "Well, maybe the car will help smooth things out."

Grady didn't think a bulldozer would smooth things out, but Charlie was already heading for the cottage. A dark bird swooped close to Charlie's hat as he walked by the gourd racks. "Hey, Marie!" Charlie called out. "You got any advice on how to handle an angry woman?" The bird swooped again and chortled at him.

Charlie laughed. "Yeah, that's what I figured."

Grady was going to open the cottage door, but Charlie stopped him and knocked instead.

When Lila came to the door, Charlie took off his cap. "I guess you're still mad at me, but I'd like to come in and talk for a minute, if you don't mind."

Lila stepped back, then stood with her hands on her hips. If she'd been wearing tall red boots, she would have looked like an Amazon Raider action fig-ure. "How am I going to stop you? You own the place."

Charlie stepped inside. "I wanted you to know I bought a secondhand car that Grady and I are going to be fixing up. I'll sell it to you for what I paid for it— a hundred dollars."

A hundred? Charlie had told him he paid three hundred. Charlie caught Grady's startled look. He shrugged and smiled.

"That's real nice," Lila said. "But I ain't never had a hundred dollars in my life, so you better sell your car to somebody else."

Grady tugged on the sleeve of her sweater. If she turned down the car, he wouldn't get to work on it. "It's a good deal, Mom. You know we need a car."

"I know I'm not giving my permission for you to be working on no car. I sure don't want you getting underneath it."

"I won't put the boy in any danger, Lila. I'll be right there with him the whole time."

Grady moved closer to Lila. "He's teaching me, Mom," he whispered. "He's teaching me to be a mechanic like Dad. He says I'm good at it."

Lila kept her action figure pose for a second, then relaxed and put her hand on Grady's shoulder. "Well, that's good, Grady. That's real good."

Charlie cleared his throat. "Listen, Lila. I've been thinking it over and I don't figure I'm paying you enough for all the work you do. I'm going to give you a twenty-dollar-a-week raise."

The Amazon Raider was back in a flash. "So in five weeks I have a free car, huh? You're prob'ly surprised I figured out the math. Me being such an ignorant piece of trash and all."

"No. Of course not. I never meant . . ." Charlie raised his hands as if he was going to say more, but then thought better of it and let them drop to his sides.

"First off, you had some nerve saying what you did yesterday, then waltzing in here with no apology and thinking a car is going to make everything all fine and dandy. I told you before, I don't take no charity."

"I'm sorry I upset you," Charlie mumbled. "I jumped to conclusions. I was wrong to do that." His shoulders were slumped, like those of a defeated man.

Lila's face softened a little. "I'm obliged to you for teaching Grady about engines. He comes by it natural. His daddy was a real good mechanic, you know."

"No, I didn't know," Charlie said. "Working with Grady is a pleasure. I never had a child in my family who was interested in fixing cars or tractors." He put on his cap, touched the brim like he was tipping it, and went out the door.

Grady was relieved that Charlie and Lila were speaking again. But in spite of all the polite words, he could still feel the remnants of his mother's anger crackling in the air like the static on a distant AM radio station.

CHAPTER
12

When Grady left the cottage the next morning, he could feel right away that the air had started to warm up. It had happened all of a sudden, as if somebody had turned the page on the calendar and, *bam*, it was spring. Flowers, the ones that Grady thought looked like they were made of wax, were pushing their heads up through the ground. Fruit trees blossomed so fast you could almost see the petals unfold, and the leaves that had only been budding on the other trees spread themselves out in the sunshine like little fans.

Charlie was outside watching his martins as Grady walked up to the big house. "See that? They're taking green leaves into the nests."

"What for?" Grady asked. "Didn't we put enough pine needles in the gourds for them?"

"The green leaves are a sign that they're starting to lay eggs," Charlie said. "They've been bringing them in for a few days now. I'm about to do my first nest check, if you want to watch."

Grady got the message. If he was only watching, this didn't count as a paid job. Seemed that nothing counted for pay anymore. But if he went through this nest check thing, it would speed things up and get Charlie working on the car sooner.

Charlie walked slowly under the gourds, studying the grass. "Now, I've been doing walk-unders every day since the birds first came back. That way if I find any feathers on the ground or other signs of trouble, I can take the rack down and see what's going on. It's important to stay on top of things. Understand?"

"Not really," Grady said. "Why do these birds need so much help from humans? Can't you put up the gourds and let nature take its course?"

Charlie looked at him for a minute, then shook his head. "You really don't get it, do you? I'll show you nature taking its course. Get in the truck."

Oh, great, Grady thought. I ask one little question, and we're off on a field trip.

Charlie pulled up in front of the cottage so Grady

could run in and tell Lila they'd be gone for a while. Grady half expected her to say no. She didn't. Then he almost told Charlie that Lila wouldn't let him go anyway, but the idea of getting off the farm appealed to him, even though he figured he'd be in for another one of Charlie's bird lectures on the way to wherever they were going.

They took off down the road in the opposite direction from town. The road was hilly and winding, passing a couple dozen small farms. Grady kept hoping they'd go through another town. The closest thing to civilization he saw was a corner with a small grocery store on one side and a gas station on the other. After about twenty minutes, Charlie pulled over in front of a farm that had the biggest birdhouse Grady had ever seen. It was covered with birds.

"Awesome!" Grady said. "It's a bird apartment house. Are those martins?"

Charlie pulled out a pair of binoculars from the glove compartment and tapped it against Grady's chest. "Here. You tell me if those are martins."

Grady rolled down the window and brought the birds into focus. "Well, some of them are martins, but the others are sparrows."

"Look again at those martins. What color are their beaks?"

"Yellow." Grady pulled the binoculars away from his eyes and looked at Charlie. "Oh, that means they're starlings, right?"

Charlie nodded. "And each pair of starlings can lay two clutches of eggs a year. House sparrows can lay three to four clutches, maybe twenty young each by the time the summer is over. The martins lay only once each season—probably four to five young at most. Who do you think will win the population race?"

"The martins should fight back," Grady said. "Why do they wimp out and let the other birds take over?"

"See those long sharp beaks on the starlings? They use them as a dagger to stab other birds in the eye. They can puncture right through a martin's brain with one jab. The martin's beak is short and wide. It's built for scooping up bugs in flight. They don't stand a chance in a fight."

Grady cringed at the thought of the starlings' attack. Still, nature was the survival of the fittest. If martins were so weak and dependent, maybe they deserved what they got. After all, he and his mother had survived without any help. Nobody built nests for them, or shot or trapped anything that might hurt them. And they were stronger for taking care of themselves. The martins could learn a thing or two from the Flood family.

Grady didn't try to argue with Charlie on the way home. He tuned out the lecture that droned on and on. Every now and then he nodded and said "uh-huh" to make Charlie think he was paying attention.

As soon as they got back to the farm, Charlie wanted to start the nest check. When he lowered the first rack, a couple of birds flew out of the gourds and circled overhead. Charlie unscrewed the palm-sized cap on the side of the gourd and looked inside. "I was right. Here's the first egg, see?" He moved a couple of leaves aside to reveal a small white egg, then marked something down on his clipboard. "The number on the gourd is one, so I mark the number-one square with the date and '1E,' meaning one egg. They lay one egg a day, so I may be marking down '5E' by the end of the week. Then when the eggs hatch, I'll write '5Y' for five young."

If Grady thought that trailing along with Charlie would make things go faster, he was wrong. Charlie had to stop and explain everything to him. They went through all twenty-four gourds and found eggs in a little over half of them. A couple of nests had two eggs.

Grady wondered why it was important to write everything down. He didn't ask, because that would only slow things down. But keeping quiet wasn't any help. Charlie could read his mind.

"I bet you're wondering why I'm keeping records of everything." Charlie proceeded to give a long explanation about how he would check every four days—one week for egg laying, another two weeks until they hatched, and four more weeks until the birds were ready to leave the nest. "I send the whole report in to the PMCA at the end of the season. That way they can keep track of how the martin population is growing or shifting locations."

Grady tried to pretend he was interested without sending Charlie off into new lectures. It was a delicate balance. If he asked a question, it was good for another twenty minutes. But if he looked bored, Charlie would say, "You ought to listen to this. It's important," and go on at even greater length. Grady's hands itched with the desire to work on that engine. Finally they cranked up the last gourd rack, Charlie put away his bird notebook, and they headed for the car.

"You try to start her up, Grady. I'll watch what happens in the engine. Just make sure she's in park."

Grady took his place behind the wheel, feeling important as he turned the key in the ignition. He listened to the engine noises, trying to memorize the coughing and sputtering sounds.

"Okay, turn her off," Charlie called. "I want to show you something."

Grady looked under the hood while Charlie pointed to different parts of the engine and told him how he knew which parts needed replacing.

"It's an educated guess right now. I like to start out with the smaller things to see what takes care of it. No sense in buying a big expensive part and finding out the hard way that some fifty-cent part is causing the problem."

"Couldn't Sal tell you what was wrong with it?"

"He said he tried a few things. Couldn't locate the problem." Charlie must have seen Grady's look of surprise. "What? You think because he's younger, he's a better mechanic than me?"

"No, but Sal fixes cars for a living."

Charlie snorted. "Doesn't mean a thing. I could make my living doing a lot of things I'm not good at. Plenty of people in this world do that, believe me."

Every now and then, Charlie would look up and shade his eyes, watching the birds coming and going from the gourds. Each time, Grady would try to get Charlie concentrating on the car again. He couldn't understand how anybody could have birds on the mind so much of the time.

———⋆⋆⋆⋆⋆———

But the next morning, as Grady looked out the window at the gourds, he couldn't help thinking about the new lives that were growing inside them.

"Funny how Charlie knew those birds were laying eggs," he told Lila. "And he knows exactly when they'll hatch, too. That should be cool to see."

Lila punched the bread dough she was kneading. "You turning into one of them bird-watchers, are you?"

Grady snorted. "Yeah, right." Although he had to admit he was looking forward to the next nest check to see how many more eggs had been laid and he was eager to see what the baby birds would look like.

Suddenly the crack of a gunshot split the air. Lila jumped, almost dropping the dough on the floor. "Why does that man have to kill them poor birds?"

"I think he's scaring them off more than anything. The starlings and house sparrows take off now soon as they see his gun. He hasn't hit one all week while I've been there."

"You make sure you don't get in his line of fire."

"I stay behind him, Mom. His aim isn't *that* bad."

Lila punched the dough so hard, Grady doubted it would ever rise again. "I'll be glad when that car is finished and I have enough money to buy it so we can get ourselves out of here."

Grady hated to hear Lila talk about leaving. She could hang on to a grudge longer than anybody. Now the gun was one more thing for her to hold against Charlie. "Why do you always run so hot and cold on people, Mom?"

Lila looked up. "What's that supposed to mean?"

"Well, you gush all over somebody one day, then they do or say something you don't like and you're finished with them—ready to pack up and get out."

Lila pointed a flour-covered finger at Grady. "I've had too many people in my life let me down. I'm all for givin' a person the benefit of the doubt in the beginning, but once I see their bad side, I put up my guard."

"Everybody has a bad side. Does that mean you don't trust anybody? Ever?"

Lila stared at him for a minute, then smiled. "I guess you're growing up. You're asking questions I don't have a quick answer for. I'll have to ponder on that one."

Grady hadn't told Lila about the trap. He figured there was no sense getting her all riled up about that. It would give her a third reason not to like Charlie. He decided to go up behind the barn and see what Charlie had caught.

He could hear them before he could see the trap. It was filled with house sparrows—over a dozen. All he ever saw were sparrows now. The starlings had moved on, probably because they couldn't get into those weird entrance holes Charlie had on his gourds. Grady had never seen what Charlie did with the birds he trapped. They disappeared without a trace, all but the few that Charlie left in the trap as decoys.

Grady crept closer to the cage, trying not to scare the sparrows with his movement. They were kind of cute—round and sassy looking. He could believe

Charlie when he talked about how sinister the starlings were. They looked the part of villains, with their beady eyes and long pointed beaks. But it was hard to imagine the chubby little sparrows doing any harm. Grady was pretty sure they were smaller than martins, so the martins should win easy in a fight.

Grady watched the house sparrows pecking at the bread and couldn't bear the thought that they were doomed. He'd seen his father rescue animals that had been caught in traps along the creek behind their house. His father had approved of hunting—even did it himself to get venison for the winter—but he said a trap wasn't a fair fight. It didn't take any brains or skill. Grady knew his father would have rescued these poor little sparrows. What would it hurt to let them go? He could shoo them away so they wouldn't bother Charlie's purple martins.

He went around to the front of the barn to make sure Charlie wasn't in sight. He also checked to make sure the trap wasn't visible from any of the windows in the big house. Then he went back and opened the door on the side of the trap. The house sparrows all crowded to the opposite side, some flying to the top, beating their wings against the wire. "Stop! You're going to hurt yourselves!" Grady whispered. He ran around to the side opposite the entrance, hoping to scare the birds toward the door, but they didn't seem to see the opening, still thrashing themselves against the top and sides of the cage. Finally he reached in and grabbed some of the bread, placing it outside the door of the trap. Then he hid behind the tractor. After the sparrows calmed down, the first two discovered the escape route. Still, it took several minutes before most of the others found their way out. A few were so interested in eating the bread inside the trap, they didn't even want to escape. Grady knew that Charlie would be suspicious if the decoys were gone, so he reluctantly closed the door, trapping three house sparrows inside. But now he knew that if Charlie didn't catch on, he could release a bunch of sparrows every day.

———————

Charlie mentioned the trap at lunch on Wednesday, but he didn't seem to be accusing Grady of anything. "Haven't trapped any house sparrows for the past couple of days."

"Maybe they ain't around anymore," Grady suggested, not lifting his eyes from his plate.

"Oh, they're around all right, but not going for the bait. I'll have to ask on the PMCA forum—see if anybody's got ideas for something better than bread to bait the trap. I'm doing a nest check this afternoon, if you want to come along."

"Sure."

This time Charlie had Grady fill in the numbers on the chart. Most of the compartments had at least three eggs, some four. Charlie let Grady be the one to look in each nest. "Push the leaves gently out of the way to see what's underneath. Then try to put them back the way you found them."

When they brought down the last rack, Charlie skipped over to gourd number twenty-one. He carefully unscrewed the access hole cover and peeked inside. "I thought you might be in there and ride the rack down," Charlie said in a soft voice. "Grady, look here. This is Marie."

Grady leaned in close, and at first he couldn't see anything. Then when he got at the right angle, he could see a small dark bird nestled in the bowl at the back of the gourd. She looked up as Charlie gently nudged her over to check the eggs she was incubating. There were five.

"Why isn't she scared of you?" Grady whispered. "Does she know you won't hurt her?"

"Don't go putting human thoughts into a wild bird's head, Grady. We can't really know what she's thinking, but Marie's been here for four summers now. She's probably used to having me check in on her." He smiled and replaced the cap. "You're a good little mother, Marie. See you in a few days."

Charlie opened the other gourds in order, humming softly as he did. A chill wind picked up shortly before they finished. "Let's skip working on the car today, Grady. I should check my records from last year against these. Need to look up a few things on the Internet, too. You're welcome to come inside, if you want."

Grady couldn't hide his disappointment. "No thanks. I've had enough birds for one day."

Charlie raised his eyebrows. "Suit yourself."

Grady went back to the cottage and sat for a while on the porch, watching dark clouds coming up over the next ridge to the west. He kept his eye on gourd number twenty-one. Finally he saw her. Marie came out of her gourd and swooped high over the meadow, catching bugs. She looked like a regular bird—one

Grady wouldn't have paid any attention to before. But he knew this bird. He had seen her inside her house, incubating her eggs. It was one thing to have a pet, like a dog or cat. But to have a wild thing like a bird trust you—Grady had to admit that was something special.

CHAPTER
13

Grady finally found a method for releasing the house sparrows that worked pretty well. If he threw a tarp over the top and sides of the cage, leaving the door open, the birds went toward the light and escaped right away. This worked so well the third day that all of the birds escaped. Grady was pleased with this until he realized that Charlie would see the trap completely empty and figure out that somebody had been messing with it. Grady put away the tarp and watched from behind the tractor, holding his breath until three house sparrows landed on the top, tilting their heads to look around before they finally hopped down to the baffle and then into the trap.

Grady breathed a sigh of relief. He felt a little guilty betraying Charlie, but he knew he was doing the right thing. He only wished he could set them all free. There were sure to be more house sparrows in the trap when Charlie came out, and Grady couldn't do a thing to save them. Then he thought of another plan. Why couldn't he lure the house sparrows away from the trap altogether? He ran to the cottage and grabbed a few slices of bread. There was more than they could ever eat, because Lila was so concerned about having fresh baked goods for Charlie, she baked a new loaf every morning, leaving the day-old bread at the cottage.

Grady went out the back door and tossed a few hunks of bread on the grass. He checked to make sure he was out of Charlie's line of sight from the main house, then broke up the rest of the bread and scattered it. There wasn't a house sparrow in sight, even though he watched for quite a while on the back step. Finally he gave up and went inside.

The next morning he noticed that some of the bread was gone, and there were a few sparrows gathered in the bushes. He took more bread and gently threw small chunks, trying not to scare them. Still none of the birds were brave enough to come forward.

But when Grady went outside the third day, the sparrows hopped around the grass pecking at the bread, and by the end of the week, Grady's plan was working better than he had imagined. The little flock was growing every day, and Grady knew that every bird that came to him was one less sparrow doomed to Charlie's trap.

It wasn't until the beginning of the next week that Lila discovered Grady feeding the birds. By now, the house sparrows were almost tame, flying down to grab the pieces of bread he tossed. "Oh, aren't they the sweetest little things? You're becoming a bird-watcher after all. I knew you had a tender heart under all that sarcasm."

"I'm not a bird-watcher, Mom. I'm just saving them from Charlie's trap." The words had slipped out before Grady realized what he was saying.

Lila sat next to him on the step. "He has a trap? I thought he was just shooting at 'em. I swear I don't know what's the matter with that man."

"Please don't tell him what I'm doing, Mom. No birds are getting hurt, because I've been releasing them from the trap. But if Charlie finds out, he'll be really mad at me because he thinks he's doing the right thing. You heard what he said about house sparrows. He's sure they're killers."

Lila gave Grady a long look and shook her head. "People sure do see things different, don't they? I don't see how anybody could think killing a helpless creature is the right thing to do. I don't mind you learning the car stuff from Charlie, but you better not take on any of his other fool notions."

Every time Grady heard Lila talk about Charlie, he realized how much this place was growing on him. They had been on Charlie's farm a little over a month now, and it was up to about a nine on the rating scale, even with the shooting and trapping. They went inside, and Grady reminded his mother of the one thing that would make her want to stay. "Where else are we gonna get a nice place to ourselves like this, Mom?"

"I know." Lila fingered the hem of the curtain in the front window. "When we first came here, I was thinking about painting the room, maybe making some new curtains to fancy it up a bit."

Grady jumped on the idea. "That would be great.

I think I saw a sewing machine up at the house. Probably belonged to Charlie's wife. And when the weather gets good, we could paint the outside. Maybe make the trim and shutters some pretty color. And you could plant flowers in the window boxes."

He could tell he got her with the window boxes. She had that dreamy look on her face. "Oh, that would be nice, wouldn't it? Maybe a white cottage with blue trim and purple flowers?"

"Yeah, Mom. You're so artistic and all. You could have this place looking good enough to be in a magazine . . . if we were staying here."

"Well, I suppose we don't have to go rushing right off. I mean I've never had a place I could fix up like I want it."

"So you think you could put up with Charlie for a little while?" Grady knew he was taking a chance with this question, but she seemed to be softening.

She shrugged. "I guess he's not so bad."

"I know he didn't mean nothing about Dad, Mom. Sometimes Charlie just says the first thing that comes to mind, is all."

"Well, he's a pretty easy man to work for. Not like some of them places we've been." Lila ran her hand over the wall. "Maybe I'll ask him about getting some paint for the inside when I go to the store."

———————

After lunch, Grady went along with Lila to town. The first stop was the hardware store, since Lila had convinced Charlie to give her some extra money for paint.

After looking at almost all the paint chips, taking them to the front window to see them in the outside light, Lila finally decided on a pale yellow. "It'll make a cloudy day seem sunny, don't you think?"

"Yeah, Mom. It's great." Grady was partial to blue, but he'd lost that battle in the first fifteen minutes. He gave up easily, not wanting to dim Lila's enthusiasm about the cottage makeover.

Just when Grady thought his mother had made a final decision, Lila went back to the paint chip display. "I'm just going to check a few more of them yellow chips to make sure I got the best one."

Grady gave up at that point and told her he'd wait outside. He was leaning against the truck when a bus with Addieville Central School written on the side stopped near the parking lot, spewing out half a dozen kids.

Three guys about his age were following close behind a smaller boy, taunting him. "Hey, retard!" one yelled to the kid. "What's the matter? You scared, little dummy boy?"

Grady slipped around to the other side of the truck where the cab hid him from view but he could look through the windows. He recognized the expression on the face of the victim. He had often worn that expression himself—eyes straight ahead, no sign of emotion on his face. He could almost imagine the thoughts going through that kid's mind. *Just keep walking. Don't let them see they're getting to you. Keep moving until you can see your house, then make a break for it.*

How many times had Grady played out this same scene when he started at a new school, always hoping he could make it home before he got beat up? Grady clenched his fists and stayed out of sight. Part of him wanted to take on all three of the bullies and send them running for home with bloody noses. The other part of him—the part that won—just wanted to stay out of it. It was none of his business.

He watched as the kid started running. The other guys didn't even chase him. Two of them picked up stones to throw at him and the other one yelled, "Bye-bye, sissy pants. Don't pee on yourself."

He could hear the bullies laughing as they swaggered on down the street. There was no way Grady was going to that school in Addieville. They'd have to handcuff him and drag him there in leg chains. He just wasn't willing to put up with that crap anymore.

Lila came out of the store lugging a gallon of paint and a large bag with a tray and roller in it. "I coulda used some help carrying all this stuff."

"Sorry." Grady took the bag and paint from her and put them in the truck bed.

"Don't matter none, sweetie." Lila was in a good mood.

When they stopped for groceries, Grady had a project in mind, too. He used some of his money to buy a small notebook and a mechanical pencil. He thought a long time about that pencil because it cost more than a dollar. But he made too many mistakes writing to use a pen, and it was cheaper to buy the mechanical pencil than getting a wooden pencil and one of those little twist pencil sharpeners.

Lila was humming as they walked to the truck. "Let's you and me swing by that restaurant, Grady.

Remember June and Bob? Those people were real nice to us. I'd like to tell them how we're getting on."

———·—·—·—·—·———

There were no cars parked outside the restaurant when they pulled up. Grady glanced over at Sal's garage. The truck was there. He hoped Sal didn't notice Charlie's truck and come running over to see Lila.

June came out from around the counter to give Lila a hug as soon as they got in the door. "Why, Lila, honey, Bob and I was just wondering about you, weren't we, Bob?"

Bob's head appeared in the window from the kitchen. "How's old Charlie Fernwald treating you? You 'bout ready to shoot him yet?"

"He's the one doing the shooting," Lila said. "He's going after those poor little birds. My nerves are all jangled up with the noise."

June shook her head. "That sounds like Charlie, all right." She grabbed three cups and poured coffee. Then she got a glass of milk for Grady. They settled in at a table in the empty restaurant. "You came just in time for our afternoon coffee break," June said.

Bob laughed. "Our coffee breaks come anytime somebody we like walks through the door. So, you think you'll be staying at Charlie's for a while?"

"Well, if you'd asked me yesterday, I might have said different, but now Grady and me aren't in so much of a rush to get away."

June went over to the counter and pulled a lemon meringue pie from the three-level glass display case. "I was hoping you might stay around." She cut four pieces.

"I'm paying for our pie this time," Lila said, with a hint of pride in her voice. She went on to tell Bob and June about the car Grady and Charlie were repairing.

Bob patted Grady on the shoulder. "You workin' on cars, huh? You may grow up to be another Sal Palvino."

"I'm going to be like my dad," Grady said through a mouthful of lemon. "Not Sal."

It couldn't have been more than three minutes later that June said, "Well, speak of the devil," and Sal Palvino came into the restaurant. He pulled a chair over to their table, set it down backward, and straddled it like he was riding a horse. This was Grady's worst nightmare. Here he'd worked so hard to get Lila to change her mind about leaving, and now she was a sitting duck for Sal.

"So how's it going with the car, Grady? You and Charlie got her on the road yet?"

Grady shook his head, pretending to be too busy eating to carry on any idle conversation. The sooner he finished his pie, the sooner they could get out of there.

"Well, that's going to be a nice little car when you get her going. My wife is real mad at me for selling it. She thought I was going to fix it up for her."

"Your wife?" Grady almost choked on a big mouthful of meringue.

"Yep. She's been after me to fix a decent car for her. Now that we have a baby, she needs a car with a good backseat to put the baby carrier in." He pulled a picture out of his wallet. "Here. This is a picture of little Sal."

They passed it around the table so everybody could admire it. Lila gushed about how that was about the cutest little baby she had ever seen. Grady studied the picture. The kid had a tuft of dark hair that was already starting to tumble over his forehead. So Sal was married. All this worry about him going after Lila, and he was married with a kid. And he sure wasn't going to mention his wife and show baby pictures to Lila if he was planning on going after her behind his wife's back.

Grady handed back the picture. "Cute kid." He felt like a sparrow that had been released from a trap.

CHAPTER
14

Grady took his new notebook and pencil to the car repair session the next morning. Charlie already had his head under the hood. He stood up and smiled when Grady set his notebook down on the fender. "You taking notes now?"

Grady nodded. "I want to make sure I get it right so I can remember everything."

"Well, I'm not saying you shouldn't write things down, but you can always ask me questions if you forget something."

"Yeah, I know, but I mean for after."

"After?" Charlie took off his cap long enough to wipe his forehead with the back of his hand.

"After we leave. I want to know how to repair the car if it breaks down so we don't get stuck again."

Charlie's smile faded. "Ah. Stuck like here, you mean." He bent under the hood again to tighten a bolt.

"No, I didn't mean that. I meant we probably won't stay forever, you know?" Grady noticed the sad expression on Charlie's face and added, "It's not like you need us here, right? You wanted your son to think Mom was going to work here to get him off your back."

"That's right." Charlie straightened up and jutted out his chin. "I don't need anybody. Haven't since my wife died."

"Right, you don't. Me and Mom don't need nobody neither."

"You don't need anybody."

"That's what I said."

"No, you said you don't need nobody, which means you do need somebody."

Grady stepped back, pocketing his notebook. "This is that grammar junk, isn't it?"

Charlie wiped his greasy hands on a rag. "It's not junk if your words are telling people the exact opposite of what you want to say. This is why school is important. Your mother needs to get you registered. I haven't forgotten that you lied to me about being homeschooled."

"I know." Grady took a deep breath. "Look, I'm sorry. I don't usually lie, but I can't go to school anymore."

"Why not? You're a smart kid. You should do fine in school."

"Yeah, well, I don't do fine. And there's no use talking about it."

Charlie opened his mouth as if to say something, then clamped it shut and nodded.

Every time Charlie explained something that afternoon, Grady stopped to write it down. A few times he read it back to Charlie to make sure he got it right. The car engine still wasn't making much sense. Everything was supposed to work in a logical order, but Grady couldn't seem to grasp the big picture.

Charlie put his hands on the small of his back and stretched. "I need to take a coffee break. I still have part of your mother's carrot cake up at the house. You want a slice?"

Grady grinned. "You know about the carrots and you still want to eat it?"

Charlie clapped Grady on the back as they started

for the house. "I know your mother's been sneaking healthy stuff into my food. Long as it tastes good, I don't mind."

"Everything Mom cooks tastes good, even brussels sprouts." Grady slowed his steps to match Charlie's.

"Brussels sprouts! She's not sneaking any of them into my food, is she?"

Grady laughed but didn't answer. As soon as they got into the kitchen, Charlie turned the burner up high under his dented metal coffeepot. That was the one thing he wouldn't let Lila make for him. He liked his coffee black as tar. Lila said she'd be poisoning him if she made it that way, so he made it himself.

Charlie went to the refrigerator and pulled out a carton of milk, holding it up like he was going to make a toast. "It's fresh. Don't even need to give it the sniff test, thanks to your mother. I haven't had anything growing green fuzz in this refrigerator since she arrived."

Grady smiled. He remembered listening to Lila's description of that refrigerator when she had to clean it out the first time. Green fuzz wasn't the half of it.

Charlie slid Grady's plate of cake across the table. "You need a fork?"

"Nah."

"Me neither. Cake tastes better when you eat it with your fingers." From the way Charlie eased himself down into his chair, Grady could tell his bones were hurting.

Charlie took a big bite of cake and licked the frosting off his thumbnail. "So tell me about this school business. Why don't you want to go?"

Grady sighed. He should have known Charlie wouldn't give up on the school issue. "Isn't it enough for me to read books? I'm twelve. I got all the schooling I need."

"There are laws about this, Grady. You have to stay in school until you're sixteen. Besides, don't you want to meet some kids your own age?"

Here it was—the same argument Lila used to give him until he came home with one black eye too many. Well, he might as well give Charlie the full story. "You wanna know what happens when I meet kids my own age? They start out by calling me names, then they trip me in the cafeteria so I drop my tray. Then next thing I know, they're beating the crap out of me on the way home from school. Sometimes they even do it in the school building."

Charlie pushed back from the table to get his coffee. It smelled like burned plastic when he poured it into his cup. "People don't beat you up for no reason. You must be doing something to cause it. You tend to have a bit of a mouth on you, in case you haven't noticed."

"Oh, yeah, I cause it all right. I cause it by not dressing the way they do and by talking funny."

"Why didn't you say so?" Charlie had a big smile now. "I can take you over to Addieville, and you can pick out some new clothes for school. My treat. What do you say?"

Grady pushed his half-eaten cake away. The thought of school had his stomach so knotted up, he felt sick. "You don't get it. It's not about the clothes. No matter where I go, I'm always the weird new kid."

"Well, you can't keep quiet if kids are beating you up. You have to tell the teacher. Get those ruffians straightened out."

"The teachers don't care," Grady said.

Charlie looked concerned. "I can't believe that."

"All right, that's not exactly true. When I was in third grade, there were these kids who were after me every day. I tried telling my teacher about them, but the kids found out what I had done and beat me up worse than ever. The teacher couldn't lay a hand on them and they all knew it. It's always like that."

"Look, you may have been in some bad schools," Charlie said, "but I'm sure the school in Addieville isn't like that."

Grady remembered the kids outside the hardware store. Things were no different here. "Look, I don't learn nothing—anything—in school, because I'm too busy watching my back. There's no sense to it. Now you're teaching me stuff and I'm reading books. That's better than any schooling I've had so far."

Charlie downed the last of his coffee and picked a few coffee grounds off the tip of his tongue. "I see what you're saying, Grady, but I think you ought to give school another chance. You can do anything you want in this life if you have an education. Without it you're nothing."

Grady knew Charlie meant well, but he had no idea what the real world was like. He was off on his own little planet with his birds, and he didn't have a clue.

They started back out to the car, but the weather had turned cold and now there was a steady drizzle.

Charlie was walking with a limp. He stopped before they reached the barn and rubbed his hands. "This change in the weather has my joints all swollen up. I don't think I can even hold a wrench this afternoon."

"Why don't you tell me what to do and I'll handle the tools?"

Charlie shook his head. "It's too cold and damp for me out here. Come back into the house and we'll look up some engine repair stuff on the Internet."

This sounded pretty interesting to Grady, but when Charlie turned on the computer, he went right to the purple martin forum.

"That doesn't look like car stuff to me," Grady mumbled.

Charlie was intent on reading the screen. "Give me a minute here. There's a thread about the weather to the west of us. Seems it's turning bad. They're even having snow out in Indiana."

Grady wandered around the room, trying to block out the constant stream of nonsense from Charlie, who was reading posts from other wing nuts out loud. Grady picked up a photo of a young couple in a gold frame with the names Charlie and Marie engraved on it. The woman was smiling and holding a bouquet of roses. Out of the corner of his eye, Grady could see Charlie turning to look at him.

"That's our wedding picture," Charlie said. "Marie and I were married right here on the farm. Almost made it to our golden wedding anniversary."

"How come you named the bird after your wife?" Grady asked.

Charlie swiveled around to face Grady. "I suppose you think that's a dumb thing to do, right?"

"Didn't say it was dumb. I just wondered, is all."

Charlie reached out and took the picture from Grady. He pulled the cuff of his flannel shirt over his hand and used it to polish the glass. "Marie was so full of life, it never occurred to me that she might die before me. It was as if the sun stopped shining after she breathed her last."

Grady could see Charlie's eyes start to water up. He hadn't meant to make Charlie feel bad. He wished he could take back the question.

Charlie motioned for him to pull over the other chair. "Remember I told you Roger brought me that first gourd rack soon after Marie died?"

Grady nodded, settling into his chair.

"Well, I had heard about purple martins but had

never had any interest in them. I put up the rack to please Roger. Seems I'm always doing things to please Roger. Then a few days later, I was sitting on the front porch, missing Marie and feeling sorry for myself, when I heard this cheerful sound and a bird came swooping in toward the gourd rack—not landing, but swooping in from all different directions. I got my binoculars and Roger's old bird book and when she landed, I got a good look at her. It was a female martin."

"So it was Marie." Grady had relaxed a little because Charlie was smiling now.

"That's right. She went into a couple of gourds on the rack, then flew away. I stayed out on the porch all day, watching. When she came back that evening, she had three other birds with her—two males and another female. They say that's very unusual for a female to be the first to arrive. Most often the male comes first, attracts a mate, then recruits other birds. But Marie was special right from the start. Anyway, the next day there were even more martins. Before I knew it, I was so involved watching those birds, I wasn't moping around every day. Every time I heard that sound, I'd come running outside, and sure enough, it would be Marie, flying close to the porch, almost as if she were calling me."

"So you think Marie is your wife come back as a bird?"

Charlie eyed Grady as if to make sure he wasn't being sarcastic, then continued. "Well, I guess you might say there were times I almost believed that. I found myself talking to her as if she were my Marie. But mostly I figured Marie had a hand in getting Roger to buy that gourd rack and sending that bird to me. All I know is, that little purple martin and her friends helped me come alive again."

Charlie's eyes started to tear up again. He put down the picture and turned to face the computer. "That's enough about martins for today. I think I found something you'll like."

Grady rolled his office chair over to see the screen. It was an animation of a car engine with all the parts labeled.

"See here?" Charlie pointed at the illustration. "It's what I was trying to explain to you. The whole cycle of the internal combustion engine—intake, combustion, compression, exhaust."

Grady pulled his chair in closer. "Yeah, this makes

it easier to see how the engine works than when you're looking at the actual car."

"Take your time with the Web site," Charlie said. "It explains everything. I've bookmarked it so you can find it again. Click through the pages and call me if you have questions."

Grady read every word and took notes. All of these things that were separate parts before worked together, and Grady could finally see the connections. He studied right up to dinner, not even noticing the time passing until the aroma of Lila's lasagna drifted in from the kitchen. And at dinner, when Charlie asked him some questions to test how much he had learned, Grady could answer every one.

Charlie gave him a thumbs-up sign. "I told you, boy. You're smart. Real smart."

Grady blushed with a combination of embarrassment and pride.

After dinner the rain had let up and there was still enough light left in the sky to see. Grady slipped behind the barn to check the trap. It was full of sparrows. He had just grabbed the tarp when Charlie came around the corner carrying a plastic garbage bag. "I'm glad to see my new bait is bringing in the house sparrows. There have been so many of them around lately."

Grady quickly shoved the tarp under a crate. "Yeah, there are a lot of them, all right."

"Don't think I've ever seen a year this bad," Charlie went on, "and there's one big male that's been trying to get in the gourds all day. Every time I get a clear shot, he waits for the second before I'm going to pull the trigger, then takes off. He's driving me nuts."

Why would Charlie worry about one house sparrow? There were several dozen martins nesting in the gourds now. No lone sparrow could be a match for them.

Charlie put on a pair of leather gloves and started to open the trap door. "You may not want to watch this. I wouldn't watch if I didn't have to do it."

Grady had no intention of watching. He ran all the way to the cottage, feeling sick that he hadn't gone to the trap in time to save those poor sparrows.

CHAPTER
15

Early the next morning, Grady heard Charlie's pickup go down the driveway and it didn't return until just before noon.

After they'd finished eating lunch, Grady asked, "We going to work on the car now?"

Charlie was shuffling through some papers. "Not just yet, Grady. I want to tend to this first."

Grady hung around for a while, hoping Charlie would finish up his paperwork, but he was still reading by the time Grady and Lila had cleared up the dishes, so Grady gave up and started off to the cottage with his mother.

They hadn't gone far when Charlie called from the porch. "Grady, you mind sticking around a bit? I want to show you something."

Charlie had the papers spread out on the dining room table. He motioned for Grady to sit down. "I paid a visit to your school this morning."

Grady's heart sank. These papers must be for registering him. He felt trapped.

"Did you hear me?" Charlie asked. "I said I went to your school. Sat in on a few classes."

Grady sighed. "I heard. When do I start?"

"Tarnation. Now you *want* to go? I thought you were through with school."

"Do I have a choice?"

Charlie pointed to the pile of papers. "This is your choice right here. I looked into the home schooling for you. I wanted to see what you thought of it before I brought it up with your mother."

"I'm not sure Mom would want to teach me. She's pretty busy."

"I wasn't thinking about your mother teaching you. I thought maybe I could do it." Charlie looked at Grady for a second, then turned and began shuffling through the papers. "Course if you think I'm too old to be teaching anybody . . ."

"No, of course not. You're fine. I mean . . . why would you want to do that?" Grady's guard was up.

People didn't do nice things unless there was something in it for them.

Charlie shrugged. "I'm willing to give it a try if you are."

"So you and me could do school lessons instead of me having to go to an actual school? And it's legal and everything?"

"It's perfectly legal. The lady at the school gave me the names of some other people home schooling in the area so we can meet with them for special activities—field trips and swimming sessions at the Y to fill your physical education requirements."

"That sounds good, but what about the car stuff? Will we still have time for that?"

"Not only will we have time for it, I think we can figure out a way to make it a part of your program. The work with the purple martins might qualify, too, as a science project. Especially the record keeping for PMCA."

Grady looked through the papers. "This is a lot of work for you, isn't it?"

Charlie nodded. "A fair amount."

"I don't get why you're doing it."

Charlie leaned back in his chair. "Remember I said I sat in on a few classes?"

"Yeah."

"Well, I get your point now."

"Why? What happened?"

"Let's just say an old man who talks and dresses funny gets the same treatment as the new weird kid in town."

Grady's eyes grew wide. "They beat you up?"

Charlie laughed. "No, but I saw the looks some of them were giving me, and I heard the nasty remarks. I guess they think all old people are deaf. But that wasn't the worst of it. What really got to me is the way some of those kids talk back to their teachers. I had no idea things had gotten so bad. I can see why it would be hard to learn there, especially if you're getting picked on."

Grady had a million questions he wanted to ask, but he let it go. The main thing was that Charlie *got* it. And as long as he and Lila stayed here, he would never have to set foot in a school again.

Grady ran all the way to the cottage to tell his mother about Charlie's plan to homeschool him. Lila didn't react the way he had hoped.

She put down her paint roller and stared at him. "He went ahead and got those papers without even asking me about it? Who does he think he is? He's not even related to you. Your schooling ain't none of that man's business."

"Mom, he didn't sign me up. He was just looking into it, is all. He was going to tell you about it."

"He should be *asking* me, not telling me. And just when did he plan to let me in on your big project?"

"I don't know. Probably later today when you're up at the house to cook dinner."

Lila grabbed her jacket. "I'm not waiting for later. He shoulda talked to me before he even mentioned it to you." She ran her fingers through her hair, leaving a thin streak of yellow paint across her forehead. "I'm going to give that man a piece of my mind. You're *my* son, not his."

Grady started to reach for his jacket, but Lila stopped him. "You stay right where you are. This is between me and Charlie." She slammed the door so hard, Grady's red Corvette rolled right off the shelf.

Grady waited until his mother had time to get to the big house. Then he took the back way and sneaked over to the bushes outside the picture window where he could peek inside without being seen himself. Lila was pacing, waving her arms around as she yelled at Charlie. Finally Charlie must have convinced Lila to sit down. Once they were both sitting, all Grady could see was the tops of their heads. Since he couldn't hear anything, he gave up and returned to the cottage where he waited, chewing on his knuckles.

It was almost a half hour before Lila showed up. Her eyes were red around the edges from crying. She sank into the couch next to Grady without taking off her jacket. "If you want to have Charlie teach you at home, I'm not going to stop you."

"Really? You don't mind?"

She reached over to brush the hair out of his eyes. "No, he's right. I ain't been looking after your education. I figured since your daddy and me got by without much schooling, it was good enough for you. But Charlie thinks you can be better than me and your father."

"No, I can't! I mean there's nothing wrong with growing up to be like you or Dad. He *said* that? He called Dad a bum again?"

"No, those are my words, not his. Charlie says you have the brains to be anything you want, Grady. I'm not going to stand in the way of that." She put her arm around his shoulders. "I've done my best, but I ain't been a very good mother since your daddy died."

"Sure you have, Mom. You and me have got along fine. I'm not very good at school, is all."

Lila grabbed his chin and turned his head toward her. "Now you listen to me, Grady Flood. You're smart. I know it and Charlie knows it. I ain't had a real high opinion of that man lately, but I can see that he wants what's best for you. This is the closest thing we've had to a home in a long time. So you get your schooling from Charlie from now on, hear? I don't want no arguments."

Grady was about to bust from joy inside, but he just nodded. "Okay, Mom. You're the boss."

"That's right." She poked him on the arm. "And don't you forget it."

When Grady woke the next morning, the first thing he thought of was rescuing some sparrows. He was feeling even more guilty about deceiving Charlie now that the old man was going out of his way to help him. But as Lila had said, nobody is all good or all bad. Charlie had this one blind spot about killing sparrows, and Grady could fix that by saving them. Maybe someday Charlie would see things his way.

He dressed quickly and started off without eating breakfast so he'd get to the trap before Charlie. But just as he neared the big house, Charlie came rushing down off the porch. "Come help me, Grady," he yelled. "Something's wrong."

The martins were flying overhead, circling the gourds and calling out with a harsh, alarming sound. When he and Charlie arrived at the gourd racks, Grady saw that there were some eggs on the ground.

Charlie bent down to pick up a few and turn them over in his hands. "They've been pecked."

"What do you mean?"

"Dang house sparrows. They've poked holes in the eggs. Destroyed them."

"Sparrows? Are you sure?"

"I'm one hundred percent sure. And I'm afraid we'll find more ruined eggs in the gourds." Charlie cranked down a rack and Grady helped unscrew the access lids. Most of the nests had broken eggs on the bottom.

"What do we do now?" Grady asked, barely able to speak over the lump in his throat.

"All we can do is clean out the broken eggs and make sure not one of those pests gets near another gourd. I'll sit out on the porch with my gun all day and all night if I have to. I just hope the martins will re-nest. Otherwise they made a long flight from Brazil for nothing, and it's my fault because I let them down." He started lowering the last rack. "Run into the cottage and get something to put the broken eggs in."

Grady was hoping that Charlie was wrong about the sparrows being at fault, but as if to prove Charlie's point, a big bull sparrow landed on one of the spokes of the last rack, chirping at them. Charlie banged his fist on the pole, sending it flying.

Grady was glad to get away from Charlie. He was sure his guilt was showing all over his face. Lila looked up from her painting when he came through the door. "Hi, sweetie. What's the matter?"

He grabbed a bag from the kitchen shelf and ran out without answering. What had he done? How could he have been so wrong? As he let the porch door slam, a cloud of startled sparrows rose into the air behind the cottage. The bread! He had scattered bread all over last night. He had to pick it up so it wouldn't attract any more sparrows. He ran around to the back of the cottage. The flock of sparrows sat chittering in the bushes. Grady got down on his knees, first picking up individual pieces of bread, then frantically trying to scoop them up, combing through the grass with both hands.

"How could you do that?" Grady cried out to the birds in the bushes. "I tried to save you! Why couldn't you just eat the bread and leave? Why did you have to mess with Charlie's martins?"

"Grady!" Charlie bellowed. "What's taking you so long? Come out here."

Grady froze. Charlie was calling from the front of the cottage. Before Grady could figure out what to do, Charlie came around the side of the cottage and saw him crouching in the grass with two handfuls of bread chunks.

"What in tarnation are you doing?" The voice thundered over Grady like a tidal wave. "Have you been feeding those vermin birds?" Charlie reached down and grabbed his arm, yanking him to his feet.

Lila came bursting out the back door. "Stop that! You take your hands off my boy!" She wrenched him away from Charlie's grip.

"You know what this boy of yours has done?"

Lila stood behind Grady, her arms crossed protectively over his chest. "I know he's been rescuing those poor little birds from you, if that's what you mean."

"I'll show you what Grady's rescuing has done."

Charlie motioned for them to follow him across the yard. Grady had never seen him move so fast. They had a hard time keeping up with the old man.

Grady could see that Charlie had cranked down the third rack—the one with Marie's gourd.

"Did they get her eggs?" Grady asked, afraid he already knew the answer.

"You look, boy. You tell me."

A thick tuft of dried grass stuck out of the entrance hole. Grady unscrewed the access lid. The gourd was packed solid.

"Pull out the grass," Charlie ordered.

The grass was jammed so tight, it was hard to get a grip on it. It wasn't until the third handful that Grady saw the dark feathers. He frantically pulled away the last of the grass to uncover her, but she didn't move.

"Take her out, Grady."

Grady lifted Marie out of the hole. She weighed almost nothing in his hand. "You didn't say house sparrows could kill the adults," he whispered. "Why didn't she get away like the others? And why did they pile all of this stuff on top of her?"

"House sparrows take what they want, and it looks like this was the gourd they wanted. Marie didn't leave because she was protecting her eggs, I imagine. We can only hope they killed her before they built the nest on top of her. Otherwise she died by suffocation. Not a pretty way to go."

A sob caught in Grady's throat. "Her eggs look okay. Can't we put them someplace warm till they hatch?"

Charlie pulled out one of the eggs and held it in front of Grady's face. There was a hole poked in it. "This egg look okay to you?"

"Grady didn't mean no harm," Lila said. "He felt sorry for the sparrows. He didn't know."

Grady felt as if Charlie's fierce glare was drilling right into his skull. He had to look away.

"Really," Lila repeated in a small voice. "Grady didn't know any better."

"Oh, he knew better, all right," Charlie said. "He just thought he knew better than me."

CHAPTER
16

Charlie came to the cottage as Lila was getting ready to go cook dinner. His face was so hard and angry, Grady almost didn't recognize him.

"I don't want you cooking for me anymore," Charlie said. "As soon as I can get that car going, I'll sign it over to you whether you have the money or not."

"I told you before," Lila said. "I don't take no charity."

"Look," Charlie said. "You can pay me later when you have the money. Or don't pay me at all. It's all the same to me. I just want you out of here. *Both* of you." He slammed the door on his way out.

Grady couldn't help himself. He ran after Charlie. "I'll help you with the car if you want me to."

Charlie didn't even turn around. "I've had more than enough of your help."

"I know you're mad at me, but it'll go faster with two people working on that car."

"Not necessarily," Charlie said, still walking. "Not if one of those two people can't follow directions."

Grady stood in the cold, watching Charlie's back, but he couldn't think of any argument that might persuade him to change his mind. It was bad enough that the house sparrows had pecked the eggs. But Marie . . . Grady knew how much that bird had meant to Charlie. And Grady had caused her to die as surely as if he had killed her with his own hands.

Grady heard the chirping of sparrows, so he went around to the back of the cottage. A good-sized flock had gathered in the bushes. They didn't look cute anymore. They started chattering louder when Grady appeared, waiting for their daily ration of bread— waiting for their friend to feed them.

Grady picked up a baseball bat–sized branch and lunged for the bushes. "Get out of here!" he yelled, thrashing blindly at the birds. The sparrows took off, but by the time he returned to the back step, they had circled around and were already settling in on the branches again. He ran at the bush over and over, scaring them off, only to have most of them return. Finally he threw the branch at them in frustration and went inside.

———————•—•—•—•—•———————

A little while later, Grady looked out the window and saw Charlie digging in the garden by his front porch. It had stopped raining, but Grady could tell it was cold because Charlie stopped frequently to rub his hands together. Grady put on his jacket and walked up to the big house. He had worked out an apology in his head, gone over it a dozen times, trying to make the words let Charlie know how bad he was feeling.

Charlie had his full attention on the digging, but Grady was sure the old man sensed his presence. "Need some help?"

"Nope," Charlie said, not looking up. He took a few more shovelfuls of dirt out of the hole, then bent down to pick up a small wooden box. He rubbed his hand over the top of it, then put it gently into the hole.

Grady had assumed that Charlie was planting something, but now he realized what was going on. "You're burying Marie?" The words caught in his throat.

"Yep."

"You got something for a marker?"

"Don't need one. I'll know where she is. That's all that matters."

"Look, I'm so sorry," Grady blurted out, forgetting every version of his prepared apology. "I mean 'sorry' doesn't even begin to say how awful I feel. I did a stupid thing. I wish it never happened."

Charlie straightened up slowly as if every bone in his body ached. "Wishing doesn't change anything, Grady. I can hardly stand to look at you anymore. Get out of my sight. I want to say good-bye to an old friend without some darn fool kid hanging around."

Grady stood there for a minute, then started walking slowly toward the cottage, hoping Charlie would change his mind and call out to him. About halfway to the cottage, he thought he could hear the old man's voice call, "Wait, Grady." He turned, but Charlie had already gone into the house. It was only his mind playing tricks on him.

Grady started running, not stopping at the cottage. Lila would want to know why he was upset, and he was in no mood for her attempts to cheer him up. When he reached the road, he crossed to the other side and kept running down a sloped field. He had no idea if he was still on Charlie's property or not, but he didn't care.

A creek cut through the lowest point of the field, just wide and deep enough to keep him from going any farther in that direction. He ran along the bank until he came to a tree stump that was cut off about the right height to sit on.

He sat there for a long time, mad at himself for messing up the only real friendship that had come his way since his father died. When his breathing slowed to a normal pace, he walked along the bank. There was a place where somebody had dumped some junk. He figured he must be off Charlie's property. Charlie might not be very good at cleaning out a refrigerator, but he wouldn't allow dumping on his land. Grady continued along the creek, picking up flat stones to skip across the deeper parts where the water was still. He chose a large flat rock and stopped himself just before he threw it. It was a perfect oval shape and a lavender color that stood out from the other stones that were mostly shades of gray. He went back to the tree stump and took the pencil out of his pocket. Lining the letters up so they would be centered on the stone, he wrote the name *Marie*, first lightly, then with dark lines when he was sure he had it right.

But that wasn't good enough. Pencil lines would be gone after the first few rains. Grady went back to the junk pile and found a small chunk of wood with the point of a nail sticking out of one side. It was the perfect tool for scraping the name into the surface of the stone. Grady knew that making a stone marker wouldn't change anything with Charlie, but it was the only thing he could think of to do. And he had to do something. He scraped furiously, concentrating so hard he didn't know how long he worked. When he finished, his writing hand was blistered in all of the spots that had rubbed against the wood.

He dipped the rock in the creek to wash away the stone dust, then wiped it on his jacket. The engraved name showed up clearly. Grady walked back to Charlie's house but couldn't make himself knock on the door. Charlie had said he didn't need a marker. Maybe he wouldn't even take it. And what could Grady say to the old man? His gift seemed foolish now. Instead of giving the stone to Charlie, Grady went into the garden and placed it over the spot where Marie was buried.

The next day, Grady kept a constant vigil by the front window of the cottage, since it was too cold to sit on the porch, but he never saw Charlie come out. He would have given anything to hear one of Charlie's boring bird lectures. If he had listened more, he might have understood about the house sparrows. Grady watched the skies, hoping to see martins, but there were none. Could this be the end of Charlie's purple martin colony?

To make matters worse, the temperature kept dropping until there wasn't a martin in sight.

Lila spent all day painting the walls. She was right about the color. The yellow paint almost made the room seem sunny in spite of the dreary clouds outside.

"Looks nice," Grady said. "Only I don't see the sense of fixing the place up. We're not going to be living here."

"I always leave a place better'n I found it. Somebody else will be moving in. I'm making it nice for them."

Grady didn't think there was much chance of Charlie hiring someone to take Lila's job. He probably wouldn't trust anybody to live on his place now.

Grady watched as Lila washed out the brush and put away the paint supplies, then filled her backpack and put the things that didn't fit into a cardboard carton.

Lila sat for a few minutes, tapping her nails on the table. Then she got up to look out the window. "How long is it going to take him to finish that car? Lord knows I want to be out of here more than he wants to get rid of us."

"It's not that easy, Mom. There's more to fixing a car than patching it up with duct tape."

"Oh, so you're the big engine expert now, are you?"

"I could be. Or could have been, if I hadn't messed everything up. Charlie was a good teacher."

Lila reached over and tousled his hair. "Don't you trouble your mind about that man. You don't have to give him another thought, hear?"

"I don't want to forget about Charlie, Mom. I don't want to leave, either." He turned to his mother. "Maybe if you asked Charlie real nice, he'd let us stay. You're good at talking people into things they don't want to do."

"Yes, I am." Lila pulled a sweater out of her backpack, refolded it, and tucked it back inside. "But I never stay where I'm not wanted, Grady. I've always made a point to get out of a place before I'm thrown out. Shoulda left here while we were ahead." She lifted her chin and smiled at him. "Don't you worry. We'll find something even better'n here. You know we will."

She did a little twirl around the center of the room, but Grady wasn't falling for her happy act. He wanted to tell her off, but the closeness of the tiny cottage made his anger seem too big to let loose, so he clamped his mouth shut and went into his room, pulling the curtain door closed behind him.

His little closet with its shelf of treasures was the only comfort Grady had left. He balanced *The Great Gilly Hopkins* on its spine and started reading the page the book chose for him. But after a few minutes, he put it on the shelf. Reading about Gilly didn't help him now. Gilly got in trouble sometimes, but what he had done was worse than anything Gilly had ever thought of doing. Now he was being punished, and he deserved it—probably deserved worse than he was getting.

Grady went to the window and watched the gourds swinging in the wind. Then he noticed something dark sticking out of one of the entrance holes. He put on his jacket and went outside. When he got closer, he could see that it was a martin wing. One of his house sparrows must have attacked again. He grabbed the winch to lower the rack. He had to hide the evidence before Charlie found out. He squinted up at the gourd. Had he seen the wing move? If the martin was injured and not dead, Charlie might know what they could do to save it.

Grady held tight to the winch handle while he thought about facing Charlie's anger. There, the wing had moved again. Or was it only flapping in the wind? He had to tell Charlie about this, even if it meant that his sparrows had killed another martin. It was the right thing to do.

He ran up the hill and found Charlie working on the car. "There's something wrong in one of the gourds. Looks like a martin is stuck in the entrance."

Charlie didn't say a word, just headed for the gourd racks.

"That one," Grady said. "See the feathers?"

Charlie cranked the rack down. The wing hadn't moved. Grady felt sick. It had to be dead. "Seems to be stuck in the entrance," Charlie said. "I can't tell what's holding him. Maybe I can give him a push from the inside."

When Charlie opened the access lid, there was a flurry of wings and several birds flew out. "Tarnation. I never saw anything like this." Grady moved in so he could see. The gourd was jam packed full of martins, piled on top of each other.

"Your hands are smaller than mine," Charlie said. "See if you can take them out one at a time without injuring them."

As Grady started to reach inside, a couple more martins flew out of the hole. Grady reached in again and cradled a bird gently in his hand. It was alive, but it made no attempt to get away. Charlie took off his cap. "Put it in here." Grady lifted bird after bird out of the gourd, placing each one carefully in the cap. He counted seven.

"There's still more in here," Grady said. "They're not all going to fit into your hat."

"Run home and get something to put them in. And tell your mother we need her help, too."

Grady ran to the cottage. "We gotta help Charlie," he gasped as he burst through the door.

Lila jumped up from her chair. "What's wrong, honey? Are you hurt?"

"I'm fine." Grady grabbed Lila's carton and dumped her stuff out on the table.

"Wait a minute! I just got it all packed."

"Some martins are in trouble. We need a box to put them in." Grady stopped at the door and turned to look at Lila. She was just standing there, not making any move to follow him. "Come on, Mom. There's poor helpless birds out there. We need you." That got her. Grady knew his mother would never pass up a chance to rescue helpless creatures.

When they reached Charlie, he was shielding his cap full of martins from the wind. He gently placed them in Lila's box and Grady carefully rescued the rest. When the gourd was empty, they carried the carton up to the house and set it on the table. That's when Charlie counted. "Fifteen martins. And that doesn't include the ones that flew off. Must have been four or five of them."

"Twenty birds in one gourd," Lila said. "Don't make sense. You got plenty of gourds for them. Why did they all crowd into one?"

"You think they were trying to get away from the house sparrows?" Grady asked, afraid to hear the answer but ready to take what was coming to him.

Charlie was lining a larger cardboard carton with newspaper. "House sparrows didn't cause this. The cold weather is to blame. My guess is that they were huddling together to keep warm. It's too cold for insects to be flying, so they're probably starving, too. I should have been paying more attention to the weather." The birds didn't make any attempt to get away as Charlie transferred them to the lined box. They had their eyes open, but they just sat there, dazed. Charlie shook his head. "I never saw a bird act like this. They must be half dead. Grady, check to see if we have any more birds in those other gourds. I'm going to call the PMCA and find out what we should do."

Grady took the empty carton and ran outside. He checked all of the gourds on the rack that Charlie had already lowered but didn't find any birds. There were none in the gourds on the second or third racks either, although several martins flew off each rack as he lowered it.

By the time he got to the house, Charlie was having Lila scramble eggs to feed to the martins. "Feeding eggs to birds don't seem right," Lila said. "It's like they're eating their own babies."

"These are chicken eggs, Mom. They probably never even met a chicken."

"The eggs are good for them," Charlie said. He

turned to Grady. "A rehabber is coming over in the morning to pick up the birds. I've ordered live crickets to be delivered. You didn't find any more birds?"

"None in the gourds. About half a dozen flew off the racks, though."

"That's good," Charlie said. "At least they're still strong enough to fly. If they come back, maybe we can save them with those crickets."

All three of them started feeding the martins. Some of the birds would take egg offered on the end of a pinky finger. Others were too far gone to eat.

"They say you need to gently pry open the corner of the beak with your fingernail," Charlie said. "My fingers are too big and I don't have any nails to speak of. You two are going to have to do this."

Grady cupped a martin in his hand. He got the beak open, then put some egg in its mouth, but the bird wouldn't do anything.

"You have to poke it down its throat," Charlie said.

Grady pushed gently at the egg. It seemed too much for the martin to swallow. He returned the bird to the box, letting the hunk of egg fall. "I can't do this. It looks like I'm going to make it choke."

Charlie picked up the martin and handed it to

Grady. "Look, they eat bugs much bigger and crunchier than these hunks of egg. Get this thought into your head, Grady. These birds are starving. You and your mother are their only hope of staying alive until morning."

CHAPTER
17

They worked on into the night. By two in the morning, several of the martins had died. Lila was so heartbroken over each death, Charlie finally sent her back to the cottage to sleep. "You go get some rest, too, Grady. I'll need your help with the cricket feeding tomorrow."

"No, I'll stay. I'll keep giving them the eggs if they'll eat them."

"All right. We can take a break, though. I'll make us an early breakfast." Charlie made coffee and poured out two bowls of cereal and milk.

Charlie slurped up his cereal, dribbling milk and a crooked line of little pastel-colored Os down the front of his flannel shirt. "Thanks for your help, Grady. I couldn't have done it alone."

"No problem."

"I think we saved the ones that are left. Did you see how they seemed to get stronger even while we were feeding them?"

"Yeah, they did." Grady was glad to see Charlie smile again.

Then Charlie's face got serious. "You know anything about that stone marker in the front garden?"

"I made it." Grady let a smile slip out, but when Charlie didn't say anything more, he held his breath, wondering if he was in trouble again.

"You and I have had our share of disagreements in the short time you've been here," Charlie said, finally.

Grady nodded. Here it comes, he thought. Making that marker was a stupid idea.

"When I saw that stone I thought it might be your work." Charlie kept his head down, pretending to pick at his ragged thumbnail. "I've been told I'm a man who holds a grudge. I suspect that's true." There was another long prickly silence, then Charlie looked up. "What I'm trying to say is . . . that was a nice thing to do. I appreciate it."

Grady felt a warm glow of relief, as if things were

getting back to normal between him and Charlie. And it seemed good to be talking about birds again. Now he was full of questions and he really wanted to hear the answers. "What's going to happen to the martins after the rehabber takes them?"

Charlie took a big swig of coffee. "The ones that live should be released here at their own colony. If the rehabber is too busy to deliver them, we'll go pick them up."

"You think they'll stay here after they're released?" Grady sipped his coffee and hardly shuddered at the bitter taste. He was getting used to it. "I still can't believe they come back to the same place every year all the way from Brazil."

"These martins will go through a lot to get here," Charlie said. "I guess home is a pretty powerful magnet."

Those words hit Grady right in the gut. "I wouldn't know about that. I never really had a home."

Charlie looked up. "What do you mean by that?"

"We haven't stayed any one place long enough to call it home."

"What about when your father was alive? You didn't move around then, did you?"

Grady shrugged. "I guess not." He always felt uneasy when his father came up in the conversation.

But Charlie kept at him. "You never told me, how old were you when your dad died?"

Grady wasn't going to say anything more, but Charlie looked at him in a way that showed he was really interested. Grady could hardly think of anyone who had ever cared about what he said or thought— except for Lila, of course. And it seemed so good to have Charlie speaking to him again, he let his guard down a little. "I don't know. I guess I was in kinder-garten. I only went to school in the morning. I know that, because in the afternoon I used to play in the dirt pile in the backyard with my trucks where I could watch my dad work on cars."

"Your mother said he was killed at work."

"He didn't go off someplace to a job. He had a garage out back where he repaired engines. He always had plenty of them to work on because he was a good mechanic. Everybody knew that. He was the best."

Grady hadn't meant to blurt out so much. Talking about his father felt good and scared him at the same time. He could feel himself moving into dangerous territory. On the only family vacation he could remember, he had stood ankle deep in the ocean. A big wave came rolling in and pulled the sand out from under his feet. He had the same unsteady feeling now.

"So he had an accident while he was working on a car?" Charlie asked.

"Yeah. He had a car jacked up and he was underneath it." Grady could picture it—his father's legs sticking out from under the car. He could see those legs clear as anything in his mind.

"Then the car dropped off the jack and crushed him?"

Grady looked up, surprised. "How did you know that?"

"It's probably the most common type of garage accident."

"Yeah, that's what happened. All of a sudden the car dropped down off the jack. Daddy kicked like anything at first. Then he went still. I ran to the car and I tried to lift up on the bumper." Just thinking about the accident made Grady's heart pound. He remembered exactly how it felt, pulling up with all his strength, the metal of the bumper cutting into his fingers, the muscles in his arms, back, and neck straining against the weight. "I couldn't lift it! I ran to the house and told Mom. She called 911, but when the ambulance got there, it was too late." Grady was so tired, he didn't try to stop the tears that came to his eyes. "It was my fault."

"Grady, if you were only in kindergarten, there wasn't anything you could do."

"But I was the only one who saw what happened." He dissolved in sobs.

"Hey, hey, take it easy." Charlie reached across the table and patted Grady's arm. "Even a grown man couldn't lift a car."

"I know! I wasted time trying to lift it. I should have run right into the house to call for help."

Charlie shook his head. "I'm sure that wouldn't have made a bit of difference. Your daddy was probably gone the second the car landed on him."

"No, he was still alive." Grady could hardly see Charlie through his tears. "I told you. He was kicking."

"That was just a reflex, Grady. If the full weight of a car drops on your chest, you're dead. Bam. End of story."

Even though Grady had gone over his father's

accident a thousand times in his head, he had never considered the fact that nobody could have saved him—that even if he had run into the house right away, it wouldn't have helped.

"I'll tell you another thing about whose fault that was," Charlie said, his voice quiet now. "You might not want to hear this, but no one should ever work under a car without having blocks under it to keep it from falling if the jack lets loose. Every mechanic knows that. Your dad was careless."

"He was not!" Grady stood up so fast, the chair tipped and fell with a bang like a shotgun. "My daddy was the best mechanic in three counties. You got no business saying he killed himself."

Grady started for the door, but Charlie got up and caught his arm. "I didn't say your daddy was a bad mechanic or that he killed himself. I'm saying he made a mistake. It wasn't your fault. None of it."

Grady pulled loose from Charlie's grip and ran out the door. The night air hit him like a pail of cold water, but it wasn't enough to douse the anger that Charlie had ignited inside him. What did that stupid old man know anyway? Who did he think he was?

Grady burst into the cabin, startling Lila, who was

sitting at the table having a cup of tea. Her cheeks were wet with tears. Grady couldn't remember the last time he had seen her cry.

"You scared me, Grady. How are the birds? You lose any more of them?"

Grady had to think for a moment what she was talking about. He had forgotten about the martins. "That's what you're crying about? Birds? I never saw you cry about my daddy, but you're crying over birds?"

Lila got up and tried to take Grady in her arms, but he pushed her away. "I want to know what happened the day Daddy got killed. Why haven't you ever told me about that?"

"I didn't want to bring up sad things, Grady." Lila used her soothing voice, the one that always made his skinned knees stop hurting. "I wanted to protect you."

"Protect me! How does not knowing what happened protect me? All this time I thought it was my fault that he died."

"Oh, honey, of course it wasn't your fault. Why would you think such a thing?" She tried to hold him again, but he shoved her arm away.

"Don't you try to make everything happy, okay? Just tell me the truth for once. Charlie said it was Daddy's own fault because he should have had the car on blocks so it couldn't fall on him. Is that true?"

"Oh, Grady, don't go digging up all those old hurts."

"Is it true? You've always made Daddy out to be some sort of saint. But if Charlie is right, then it's Daddy's fault that we have to live like a couple of bums, going from one crappy place to another."

Lila winced as if he had slapped her.

"And why don't we have family like everybody else?" Grady forged ahead, ignoring Lila's stricken expression, because if he had cracked open the trunk of demons, he might as well yank them all out into the open—ask all the questions that Lila had never answered. "Why don't we, huh? We didn't drop off a spaceship. You must have a mother and father, and Daddy's family, they must be around somewhere. There have to be aunts and uncles, cousins. Why didn't we go stay with one of them after Daddy died? Where are they now?"

Lila moved her hands as if she were trying to

explain something, but the only thing she managed to say was, "Gone. They're all gone, Grady."

"Gone? From what? A fire? Explosion? Tornado? What goes and carries off a whole family? Why haven't you ever talked about them? Because this isn't the first time I asked. You know it's not. You've always told me not to worry myself about it, but that answer doesn't cut it anymore."

Lila sat on the couch and patted the cushion beside her. "All right. Calm yourself down and sit. I'll tell you what you want to know."

She took a sip of tea, then set the cup down and folded her arms tight around herself. Grady settled in beside her.

"When I was fifteen, your daddy came into town and turned my world upside down. All I could think about was that I wanted to be with him for the rest of my life. He wasn't much older than me. He'd up and run away from home and hitchhiked himself halfway across the country, because there wasn't nobody at home who cared if he lived or died. Least that's the way he told it. He never wanted to have anything more to do with his family. He wouldn't even tell me where he came from, because he was afraid I'd try to get in touch with them—get them together again. You know how I am." She flashed a brief smile, then pulled her sweater tighter around herself.

"Okay, so that's Daddy's family. But what about yours?"

Lila tried to take another sip of tea, but the cup was empty. "My parents didn't like your daddy. Didn't like him one bit."

"Why not?"

"I truly never understood that, Grady. Pa said he was nothin' but a bum. Told me I wasn't to see him anymore. But we did see each other. And before we knew what was happening, we fell in love."

She rubbed the thin gold wedding band on her finger. "Then one night we decided we was going to run off and get married. When Arlan and me went to tell my folks, Pa went to the mantel, took down my school picture—the one where Ma pasted in the pictures of me from every year since kindergarten—and he threw it in the fireplace. Then he looked me straight in the eye and said, 'I have two sons, but I ain't never had a daughter.' Said it so cold and mean, I felt like I was nothin'."

Grady realized he had been holding his breath. He let it out in a big puff. "You never tried to see them again? Make your pa change his mind?"

"Weren't no use, Grady. You didn't talk back to Pa. I knew Ma was upset because she started crying, but she didn't stick up for me. Neither did my brothers. From that moment I was dead to all of them."

Grady let it all sink in. There really wasn't anybody but him and Lila. That's when he knew that in the back of his mind, he had always held the faint hope of a family somewhere—people who cared about them, who would have taken them in, helped them, if they only had known where Grady and Lila were. He swallowed to push down the feeling of emptiness left behind by that phantom family. And now even the golden memory of his father was faltering. He was almost afraid to ask the hard question again, but he had to know. "You still didn't tell me about Daddy's accident. Was it his own fault, like Charlie said?"

Lila nodded. "I guess it was, in a way. Your daddy was trying to get a job done fast and he took a shortcut. He did something foolish and left me to take care of you with no money. He was a good man, Grady. He never meant for you and me to be like this. I did the best I could. I thought if I pretended everything was all right . . . but I never knew you blamed yourself. Oh, honey, I'm sorry." She looked as if she might start crying again, so this time it was Grady who comforted her.

"It's okay, Mom," he said, in his own version of a skinned knee voice. "We've never gone hungry and we never had to sleep out in the cold. You did all right."

"*We* did all right, Grady. You and me. Half the time the only thing that kept me going was you, knowing I couldn't fall apart because I had a son to look after. Now that you're older, I notice you do your share of watching out for me, but I'm not the delicate flower you think I am."

"I never called you a delicate flower."

"You know what I'm talking about. You think every man we run into is after me."

"Well, they *are*, Mom! Don't you see the way they look at you?"

"Yes, I do, but you see me lookin' all googly-eyed back at them?" Lila made a goofy face.

"No, I guess not."

"All right, then." Lila got serious again. "And I want to get something else straight. Don't you dare think I haven't shed tears over your daddy. I always waited till you were asleep and then I sobbed my eyes out. They were heartbroken tears at first. Then later they were angry tears, because I was madder than a wet hen at that man for leaving us alone in the world. But I'll always be grateful to your daddy for giving me the best present I ever got in my whole life."

Lila took Grady's face in her hands and wiped the tears from his cheeks with her thumbs. "You."

CHAPTER 18

Grady woke up the next morning to the sound of clattering dishes. Lila was fixing herself some breakfast. He was on the couch, with a blanket over him. "I didn't mean to wake you, honey," she said. "You seemed comfortable enough on the couch last night, so I let you stay there. I thought I might wake you if I pulled down my bed, so I slept on your cot."

Grady jumped up. "But I didn't want to sleep. I was going back to help Charlie feed the birds. Where's my jacket?"

"First you're going to feed yourself. Besides, there's no rush because those birds left about half an hour ago with the rehabber. I watched from the window—saw her put the carton in her truck."

"Charlie's going to need me to toss crickets to the

birds that are left." Grady found the jacket and headed for the door.

"Wait. Take this with you." Lila spooned her scrambled eggs onto a piece of toast, squirted some ketchup on it, and plopped another piece of toast on top to make a sandwich. "Looks like one of them Egg McWhatsits," she said, handing it to him.

"Okay, Mom. Thanks."

A cold wind hit Grady as soon as he stepped outside. He turned up the collar of his jacket and munched on his breakfast sandwich as he trudged toward the big house. What was the matter with the weather around here? It was supposed to be spring. Grady gulped the last bite and licked the ketchup off his fingers as he climbed the porch steps. Charlie must have seen him coming because he opened the door before Grady could knock. "So, you got over being mad at me?" Charlie asked.

Grady kept himself hunkered down in his jacket. "Pretty much. You got over being mad at me?"

Charlie nodded. "I'd say so. We don't have time for arguing. Soon as those crickets get here, we'll have our hands full. I told the rehabber we were going to try feeding the martins that are still around. She says it's a good idea. People out in the Midwest have saved whole colonies that way."

"Did you lose any more birds after I left?"

"No. I made sure they'd all had something to eat, then I went to bed. They looked a little better this morning. The rehabber said we probably saved their lives with the eggs."

Grady had a million questions, but he didn't have a chance to ask any of them because a UPS truck pulled into the driveway.

"That's what we've been waiting for, Grady. Run ahead and get the package so he doesn't have to come up all the way to the house. I'll meet you down by the gourds."

The driver was getting out of the truck as Grady reached him. He held a box at arm's length. Two sides were open with screen stapled to them. "So what do you use these crickets for anyway?" he asked. "Are they some kind of bait?"

"We're feeding birds. Purple martins. They're starving because of the cold weather."

The driver saw Charlie limping along the driveway. "Well, you and your grandpa have a good time, kid. I'm sure those birds will appreciate the meal.

And I'm going to appreciate the peace and quiet in my truck. That chirping drove me nuts."

Grady could feel the vibration of tiny feet skittering around inside the box. It hardly weighed anything. He thought over what the UPS guy had said about Charlie being his grandpa. Neither of his real grandfathers cared for his own kid, much less a grandson.

Charlie came up to him, huffing and puffing. He pointed up at the racks. "Looks like we got some company."

There were seven martins on the perch above the first gourd rack. Grady had been so busy thinking about grandfathers, he'd never looked up.

"Let's get started." Charlie slit open the top of the box with his penknife and pulled out an egg carton. It was square, to fit the box, and several more egg cartons were stacked under it.

"You got eggs?" Grady asked.

"Nope." Charlie lifted the lid to reveal compartments filled to the brim with shiny black insects.

"Holy mackerel. There must be dozens of them in here."

"Better be a thousand altogether," Charlie said. "That's how many I paid for."

"You ordered a thousand crickets for seven birds?"

"That's how they come. What did you think? I could order seven purple martin Happy Meals? Anyway, we might get more birds before this is over. I'm betting we'll use them up." Charlie picked a cricket out of the tangled mass and shook it to unhook a couple of others that were clinging to it. Then he threw it up toward the rack. It stopped several feet short of its mark and dropped to the ground. "Heads up! Here comes breakfast," Charlie called, tossing another and another, but he couldn't get them high enough. The birds hunched on their perch, ignoring the spectacle below them.

"You gotta throw them higher," Grady said.

Charlie gave him a look. "No, you think?" He shook his head as he bent down to untangle another cricket. "Boy's a genius," he muttered.

"Look, you don't need to get sarcastic. I'm trying to help."

"You can help by finding those three crickets I tossed."

"Oh, yeah. That's really important, because if we only have nine hundred and ninety-seven crickets, one of these birds is going to starve for sure."

"Are you two going to keep yammering at each

other, or are you going to help them poor birds?" Lila had come up on them while they were arguing.

Grady picked a cricket out of the box and tossed it as high as he could, but the wind took it and it went way to the left of the rack.

"Not as easy as it looks, is it?" Charlie said.

"Never said it looked easy."

"What you got to do is get it right up there in front of them so they see it," Lila volunteered.

"Okay, you try it, Mom."

"Oh, I was never very good at sports in school."

Grady zinged another that went off course. "Was cricket tossing a big sport in your school, Mom?"

Lila laughed. "Grady, you know what I mean. I could try." She reached into the box, then pulled her hand out. "They're still alive!"

"That's the way it happens in nature," Charlie said. He had given up on tossing and was rubbing his shoulder.

Grady held a cricket out to Lila. "I could kill this one for you. Want me to wring its neck?"

"Grady Flood! You stop talking like that. I'm not touching one of them crickets, dead or alive." Lila turned up the collar on her jacket and shuddered. Grady wasn't sure if it was from the wind or the crickets.

"All this talk isn't helping the birds," Charlie said. "Keep trying, Grady. My shoulder has nearly given out, and your mother isn't taking to the project, so you're the one who has to figure out how to do this."

"All right." Grady searched the box for the biggest cricket, thinking its weight might make it fly in a straighter line. It didn't fare much better, still veering off to the left with the wind.

"You have to compensate," Charlie said.

"I have to what?"

"Compensate. You have to figure what the wind will do and aim accordingly. Did you ever play golf?"

"Oh, sure," Grady said, rolling his eyes. "We had a championship golf course on the commune. Tiger Woods used to play there all the time."

Charlie picked up another cricket. "What I mean is, you know the wind will carry it off to the left, so aim to the right of the birds. Then maybe the wind will put it right in front of them." Charlie made an attempt at a toss, but the cricket never got any height at all and dropped at the base of the pole.

"Yeah, I see what you mean," Grady said, then immediately felt bad about his smart remark when he saw that Charlie was really in pain from his shoulder.

"We need something to make the crickets go faster,"

Grady said. "Sort of a cricket rocket launcher." He remembered the plastic toy he'd been playing with at the grocery store. "Like a slingshot. You got one, Charlie?"

"I used to make them when I was a boy. All you need is a fat rubber band and a forked branch. I might have some of those wide rubber bands in the junk drawer by the sink. You're using that brain of yours now, Grady. I think speed is the answer. We need to really propel those things up there. You run up and look for the rubber bands and I'll find us a good branch."

Grady headed for the house, surprised at how good it made him feel when Charlie gave him a compliment. The junk drawer was well named. It had pencil stubs, unmatched shoelaces, and empty key rings from things like Keystone Farm Days and fertilizer companies. There was a bunch of plastic forks and spoons Charlie used to eat his frozen dinners with before he had Lila to cook and do dishes for him. The creepiest thing was a single leather work glove with holes worn through the ends of the fingers and so stiff from dirt it looked like it still had a hand in it. There was everything but fat rubber bands. Grady started to close the drawer but had to open it again to squash things down so it would close. That's when he got this great idea. He grabbed what he needed out of the drawer and ran to the gourd rack.

Charlie was cutting notches in a forked branch. "You find the rubber bands?"

"I found something better." He held up his treasure. "Plastic spoons."

"You think you're going to spoon-feed them birds, Grady?" Lila asked.

"Nope. Watch this." Grady put a cricket in the bowl of the spoon, pulled it back, and let it fly. It went several feet above the birds' heads.

"That's it!" Charlie said. "Give me one of those spoons. I can do that." Charlie's cricket zinged right by one bird's head. The bird turned to look as it went past. "We're getting their attention. Come on, birdies. Let's see you catch your breakfast."

Grady's next shot went above and in front of the birds on the highest perch. All seven little heads followed it, like spectators at a tennis match.

"This is going to work, Grady," Charlie said. "Keep them coming right there. How did you think of this? How did you know you could use a spoon as a catapult?"

"Easy." Grady reloaded and let loose. "Food fights in school."

"You slung your perfectly good food around at people?" Lila asked.

"Heck, no. I was the target."

Charlie glanced over at Grady. "You've got mighty good aim for somebody who was only the target."

Grady grinned and shot again. This time one of the birds left the perch and went after the cricket, snatching it up before it hit the ground. "Did you see that? He got it!"

They kept firing. About ten more shots went unclaimed before two more birds got the idea and dove for crickets. Then it was as if the word was out. Each time Grady or Charlie launched a cricket, all seven of the birds flew after it. "It works!" Grady shouted. "They're eating! Come on, Mom. Help us!"

Lila gingerly placed a cricket on her spoon. "I'm sorry, little cricket. You're giving your life for a good cause." Her aim was good. The cricket was snapped up in a flash.

Gradually they settled into a rhythm with the birds. All three shot at the same time. The birds would swoop for the food, then circle around to the perch, waiting patiently for the next launch. The birds got so smart they started taking off as soon as they saw the spoons pulled back.

One time when Grady dropped his cricket and yelled, "Wait!" the birds bolted like runners off the block before the starting gun.

They kept launching for the next twenty minutes.

"I wonder what these crickets are thinking?" Grady asked. "I mean one minute I'm this little black bug crawling around, hanging out with my friends. Then all of a sudden I'm zinging through the air. And I'm yelling, 'Hey, Ma, look at me! I'm flying!' Then zap! I'm toast!"

"Grady, that isn't funny," Lila said.

But Charlie was laughing. "Yes it is, Lila."

Suddenly Grady noticed it wasn't the seven birds anymore. "Look! There must be twenty of them up there now."

Charlie put his hand on Grady's shoulder. "Well, I'll be. They're coming in from other colonies."

"Why would they do that?" Grady asked. "Didn't you say they always return to their own home?"

"Yes," Charlie said, "but maybe they figure home is where people care about what happens to them."

Lila was happily launching crickets now. "It's a miracle, isn't it? It's like they know we're trying to help them. They must have gone and told their friends."

More and more birds swirled overhead as Grady, Charlie, and Lila sent breakfast up to them.

"It's going to be a good year," Charlie said. "The weather is supposed to break in the next few days. That's still plenty of time for these martins to renest. Wait till you see the young birds when they first start to fly. The adult birds all gather around to cheer them on. It's a sight you'll never forget."

"You want us to stay long enough to see that?" Lila asked. "You don't want us to leave?"

"What's past is done," Charlie said. "I'd be pleased to have you two here as long as you want. That is, if you want to stay."

Lila smiled. "It's okay with me if it's okay with Grady."

Grady shrugged. "I don't care."

"Oh, really?" Charlie raised his bushy eyebrows. "Don't care one way or the other?"

Grady ducked his head and grinned. "Well, maybe a little."

Charlie pretended to punch Grady on the arm. "Aw, now you're going all mushy on me. Let's cut out the chatter and feed our birds." Charlie loaded his spoon and launched another cricket.

Grady stopped for a minute to take in the scene around him. The martins swooped and circled, filling the air with their excited chortling. Grady felt a weight lift from his shoulders. If he could sprout wings, he'd be soaring through the air—like a purple martin who had finally made the long flight home.

Author's Note

Any mention of sparrows in this book refers only to house sparrows. There are many species of native sparrows in North America, none of which will nest in purple martin housing or interfere with purple martins in any way. It is only the non-native house sparrow, introduced to North America from Europe in the late 1800s, that destroys purple martin eggs and young. As a non-native species, the house sparrow is not protected.

GOFISH

MJ AUCH

What did you want to be when you grew up?
A ballerina, an artist, or a veterinarian.

When did you realize you wanted to be a writer?
I had always thought of myself as an artist until I took a weeklong writer's workshop with Natalie Babbitt. When she said she discovered she could paint better pictures with words than paint, that struck a chord with me, and I've been writing ever since.

What was your worst subject in school?
Algebra.

What was your first job?
Designing fabric prints for men's pajamas in the Empire State Building—but only on the fifth floor.

How did you celebrate publishing your first book?
After two years of rejection, I sold my first two novels to two different publishers in the same week. I don't remember any specific celebration, other than being deliriously happy!

Where do you write your books?

I use a laptop, so I can write anywhere. One of my favorite places is on a train, because watching the scenery pass by seems to kick my brain into creative mode. I also like to write on our front porch when weather permits.

Which of your characters is most like you?

There's a little of me in all of my main characters. They all carry my value system and sense of justice.

When you finish a book, who reads it first?

Members of my two critique groups hear the book as I'm writing it. We're lucky to have some wonderful children's writers in our area. Each group meets once a month and we all drive up to an hour to get together. I get valuable early input from writers I respect and trust—Tedd Arnold, Patience Brewster, Bruce Coville, Kathy Coville, Cynthia DeFelice, Alice DeLaCroix, Marsha Hayles, Robin Pulver, and Vivian Vande Velde. The main person I count on is my editor, Christy Ottaviano, who pushes me to take the story far beyond the point I could go alone.

Are you a morning person or a night owl?

I'm a little of each, so I probably don't get enough sleep. I try to write every day when I first wake up, as long as it's after 5 AM. Then I have a tendency to fall asleep watching late-night TV. I guess that makes morning my more productive time.

What's your idea of the best meal ever?

Any meal eaten with good friends.

Which do you like better: cats or dogs?

I was raised with cats as a child, and although I still enjoy them, it has been dogs that have captured my heart. Our last three dogs have been rescues. It gives me and my husband, Herm, great pleasure to take in a dog that has had a tough life.

What do you value most in your friends?

Two things. First is honesty. I don't like people who play mind games. I like to know straight out what they're thinking. It's hard to have any kind of relationship when people don't tell the truth.

Second but equal is a sense of humor. I admit to being a humor snob. I like people who are spontaneously funny. I'm lucky to have a large group of friends who fall into that category. There is always humor crackling around the room when we get together.

What makes you laugh out loud?

Spontaneous funny conversations with friends. Spending time with genuinely humorous people gives me much more pleasure than so-called professional comedians.

What's your favorite song?

I love playing and singing old jazz standards. Some of my favorites are "Moonlight in Vermont," "A Nightingale Sang in Berkeley Square," and "A Foggy Day in London Town."

What are you most afraid of?

Fire, which was probably what drove me to write *Ashes of Roses*.

What time of the year do you like best?

Fall, especially in the Northeast. It's the one season that doesn't last long enough. I never tire of the reds, golds, and brilliant oranges of the fall foliage.

If you were stranded on a desert island, who would you want for company?
My husband. He's my best friend and soul mate.

If you could travel in time, where would you go?
I'm happy with the years my life has spanned so far. I grew up in simpler times, back in the forties and fifties, and now I get to experience the amazing technological advances we have today. There are many earlier periods that interest me, but I wouldn't want to visit them because of the discomfort factor. They'd be smelly and buggy!

What's the best advice you have ever received about writing?
Don't talk about writing. Just sit down and do it.

What do you want readers to remember about your books?
I hope that they carry the characters with them for a long time and consider them to be friends.

What would you do if you ever stopped writing?
There are lots of other things I enjoy doing. Music is a big part of my life. I love singing three- or four-part harmony. If I weren't a writer, I'd probably be a backup singer. I also enjoy playing string instruments—guitar, banjo, mandolin, and fiddle. I'm not very good at any of these, but I love the challenge of trying to get better.

Other hobbies include designing and sewing clothes. I do this mostly for myself, although I made most of the costumes for our daughter's medieval wedding, and it's fun sewing the costumes for the chickens in our picture books.

I wish I had the time for some serious, non-book-related painting. I was an art major in college, and love doing abstract oils on large canvases.

What do you like best about yourself?
The fact that I'm honest. It gets me in trouble sometimes. I try to be tactful, but I always tell the truth. I think it makes me a friend who can be trusted.

What is your worst habit?
Procrastination. I'd be a lot more productive if I could keep myself from going off on tangents instead of staying focused.

What do you consider to be your greatest accomplishment?
I don't know how much credit I can take for this, but Herm and I raised two wonderful and talented children. They're now both artists in their own right—Kat, a freelance graphic and magazine designer, and Ian, an interactive and motion graphics designer working in advertising. They both have turned into genuinely good human beings.

What do you wish you could do better?
Everything! I love to learn new things, so I'm always working on something—right now it's playing jazz guitar—but I'm always frustrated that I don't progress as fast as I'd like.

What would your readers be most surprised to learn about you?
That I hated history in school. All they had us do was memorize dates of battles. That's why I like to write historical fiction, so I can make a period from the past come to life.

Keep reading for an excerpt from

MJ Auch's **One-Handed Catch,**

coming soon in paperback from Square Fish.

EXCERPT

"Hey, Norm, you gotta see this."

My best friend, Leon, had his face pressed up to the screen door of our family meat market. I was supposed to be stocking shelves, so I glanced over to see if Dad was watching. He was waiting on a customer as I slipped outside.

"What's the big deal?" I asked.

"You'll see. Over here, behind the garbage cans."

I followed him.

Leon opened a paper bag. "Fireworks for tonight. Not just sparklers and snappers, either. These are the good ones." He held up a cardboard cylinder with a stick coming out of the bottom. "Get a load of this."

"Wow, is that a rocket? The kind that explodes way up in the air?"

"Sure is. I got three of them. And a couple of cherry bombs, too. If you come over, we can set them off behind the school after it gets dark."

"Where did you get all this?"

"My cousin, Bill. I have to give him my allowance for the next three weeks to pay for them. You should see all the stuff he has. He and his friends are driving out to the lake tonight to set them off."

"This is great!" I said. "I can't believe we get to see fireworks again." I had only been six years old when the war started, but I could still remember fireworks. They were banned all during the war because of the blackouts. We couldn't even have firecrackers because the flame from a match might be seen from the air. Once, during a drill, I had opened our blackout shade just a slit to peek out. Our neighborhood air-raid warden saw it and gave me holy heck.

I was glad Leon had fireworks, but I wasn't going to stand close to him when he set them off. Leon was a good friend, but he didn't always think things through. "You sure you know how to do this?"

"It's a cinch. You just set them up and light the fuse. Bill told me how."

I could picture Leon lighting the wrong end of something and blowing us to smithereens. "Maybe we should take your stuff to the lake with your cousin."

"First off, Bill doesn't want us hanging around, because he'll have his girlfriend with him. Besides, my sister would never let me go if she knew they were doing fireworks. Our mom always used to tell us you can blow your hand off with these things." Leon lived with his father and his older sister, Phyllis, who was supposed to keep track of him.

"Yeah, my mom says the same thing," I said. "She wouldn't let me go, either. I gotta get back to work, Leon. I'll come over to your house after dinner."

I tried to keep the door from squeaking as I went back in. Then Mrs. Baumgartner came barreling in right behind me and let it slam. Dad looked up from behind the meat counter in the back, but I ducked into the canned vegetable aisle before he saw me. I had just opened a case of canned corn before Leon had called me outside. Now I moved the cans of corn on the shelf to one side and checked the new price that Mom had written on the case. I marked the new cans with a grease pencil and pushed them to the back of the shelf. It was two cents more than before, so I had to wipe off the price on the old cans and re-mark them before stacking them in front of the new stuff.

Mrs. Baumgartner came down my aisle. "Good morning, Norman. I'll take one of those cans before you raise the price. Eight cents is more than enough to pay for corn." Mrs. Baumgartner was always looking for a bargain.

"Yes, ma'am," I said, handing it to her. Dad's rule was that the customers are always right, even when they're wrong, so I didn't argue with her.

I finished up the corn and went to get a carton of canned peas from behind the meat counter. Mrs. Baumgartner was looking in the display case with a scowl on her face. "Your chicken livers are fifteen cents a pound, Walter? That's highway robbery. Morton's Grocery had them for ten cents this morning."

My father was wrapping hot dogs. "Then why didn't you buy chicken livers from Morton, Mrs. Baumgartner?"

"Because he was out of them, that's why."

Dad tied string around the package and slid it across the glass to his other customer. Then he leaned on the counter and smiled. "When I'm out of chicken livers, Mrs. Baumgartner, I sell them for a *penny* a pound."

Mrs. Baumgartner looked huffy for a second, then almost smiled. "All right, Walter, give me a half pound of your gold-plated chicken livers."

That's why everybody liked Dad. He could always joke people out of their bad moods. I would have told old Mrs. Baumgartner to go fly a kite, which is why I didn't have to wait on customers very often. I liked stocking shelves because I could be a million miles away, thinking about things I'd rather be doing, like drawing pictures of cars or playing baseball, the same as I did in school. Last year, my fifth grade teacher, Miss Dworetsky, nicknamed me "Dreamin' Norman" because I was always off in my own world. She also called me "Norman Rockwell" because anytime I wasn't daydreaming, I was doodling in my notebook.

When I grow up, I want to be either a baseball player or an artist, but I've never told my family. Dad thinks I'll work full-time in the family business after high school. He's always telling Mr. Knapp, the sign painter, that he'll need a "Schmidt and Son" sign painted one of these days. Heck, I could paint that sign myself, if I wanted to work here, which I don't.

The screen door slammed every couple of minutes now. People were coming in to get hot dogs and chopped meat to make hamburgers for their Fourth of July cookouts. Dad had the chopped meat on special for the holiday—fourteen cents a pound. I supposed Mrs. Baumgartner would want that for less, too.

This was the first Independence Day since the war ended, so people were celebrating in a big way. Meat rationing was over. Now people could buy as much as they wanted, so they went hog wild.

We had a line of customers that wound from the meat counter to the potato chips and pretzels up by the front door. Ray, our only employee, was ringing up sales every few minutes. Usually Mom would have been helping Dad wait on customers, but she had taken my younger sister, Ellie, to march with her Brownie troop in the Fourth of July parade. If Dad didn't need me in the store, I'd be marching, too, with my Boy Scout troop. Ellie got off easy. She hardly ever had to do store work.

"Norm," Dad called. "Give me a hand back here."

I thought I'd get stuck waiting on customers. That's not why he wanted me, though. "I'm running low on chopped meat. I need you to make me some."

"Sure, Dad." What a relief. I didn't get to use the meat grinder very often. If I worked for somebody else, I probably wouldn't get to use it at all. But in a family business, everybody did what was needed, no questions asked. Dad had taught me how to use the meat grinder when I was nine.

Dad brought out a heavy tray of beef chunks and set it on the thick wooden table that had the grinder bolted to it.

"Call me as soon as you're done with this, Norm. I need it—*mach schnell*. We're selling more chopped meat than I expected."

I started the motor, filled the tray on top with beef, and pushed the pieces over so they fell though the hole in the tray down into the hopper. From there, a steel corkscrew grabbed the meat and moved it through a long tube. At the end, it was sliced by a rotating blade and pushed through a plate that had small holes.

Ever since I was a little kid, playing in the back room while my parents worked, I had liked to watch the meat come out of the grinder. The long, thin ropes of beef looped back and forth over themselves like the yarn wig on Ellie's Raggedy Ann doll.

I shoved the meat down into the hopper with a wooden plunger, then refilled the tray. I didn't mind missing the parade. It looked like rain. I hoped it wouldn't rain tonight, though. The fireworks might be hard to light if they got wet. Maybe they'd just fizzle. Boy, that sure would be disappointing.

The grinder motor slowed down, so I poked with the plunger, but it didn't help. I could see a piece of gristle that had gotten caught in the corkscrew. I grabbed the end of it and tugged. I must have loosened whatever was caught, because the hunk of gristle suddenly tugged back—hard.

I'm not sure when I realized that I couldn't pull my hand out. Whenever it was, it was too late. I don't know why I didn't flip the switch. I guess my brain couldn't believe what was happening. Dad had asked me to give him a hand, and that's exactly what I was doing. I was fast becoming part of the fourteen-cent chopped meat special—which, I'm told, was not a big seller for the rest of the day.

I must have screamed bloody murder. Dad came running in and turned off the grinder. He looked into the hopper, but didn't even try to pull my hand out.

He yelled to Ray. "Call Dr. Cupernail. Norm's been hurt bad."

Some of the customers rushed in to help. A woman asked me if she could get me something. I said the first thing that came into my mind, "A cherry soda from Sager's, please." She ran two doors down to Sager's soda fountain and brought the drink back in a glass with ice. It tasted cold and sweet. I didn't feel any pain, but I must have looked pretty bad, because Ray stepped behind my stool and stood with his arms wrapped tight around my middle to hold me steady.

Dr. Cupernail arrived fast. At least I think it was fast. Time was doing funny things in my head. He was our family doctor and lived nearby, so he knew the way. "Well, Norman, what have you gotten yourself into here?"

"A meat grinder," I said.

"I can see that." Dr. Cupernail put his medical bag on the table and took off his suit jacket. He was a big man, and sweating from the rush of getting here. He got serious when he looked down into the hopper. "You tell me if anything hurts, Norman." He pressed gently on my arm, starting at the elbow.

"Feel any pain?"

"No."

He pressed lower on my arm and looked at me. "Now?"

I shook my head.

He rolled up his sleeve and moved farther down. "How about now?"

"It doesn't hurt."

"I'm just going to see if I can wiggle your hand around a bit and get you out of this. You be sure to tell me if I hurt you."

He worked at it for a few seconds, then gave up.

"I didn't feel it," I said.

Dr. Cupernail patted my shoulder. "That's all right, Norman."

"We can take the whole grinder apart," Dad said. "Maybe he's caught his finger in the corkscrew."

Dr. Cupernail adjusted his glasses and looked closely at the end where the meat comes out. "Walter, I'm not going to try to get Norman out of this. The way he's clamped in there is keeping the bleeding under control. We'll let them extricate him in surgery. The boy's going into shock, so we need to get him to the hospital right away. Can we detach the grinder in one piece from the motor?"

"Sure. It all comes apart." Dad's voice was funny—low, like he was trying not to cry. Dad never cried.

"You think they'll let me out of the hospital by dinner?" I asked. "I have plans for tonight."

Dr. Cupernail checked my heart with his stethoscope. "Let's take things one at a time, Norm. Just one thing at a time."

I was kind of in and out after that. Some guy told me, "Don't worry, kid. Everything's gonna be okay."

I knew it wasn't going to be okay. Don't ask me how, but I knew. I leaned back against Ray and closed my eyes. I heard the familiar sounds of the grinder being taken off the motor. We did it at least twice every day to clean it. That was another one of my jobs. The thing weighed about forty pounds, so Dad always had to lug it over to the sink for me.

When they finally got the grinder loose, Dad and Dr. Cupernail carried it between them, while I walked close behind it. Ray couldn't go with us. He had to stay and run the store. As we passed him I reached out to stop Dad and the doctor. "Wait! I gotta tell Ray something."

"What is it, Norm?" Ray asked, leaning close.

"Whatever you do, don't sell that chopped meat I made," I whispered. "You gotta do a new batch."

Ray had tears in his eyes. "Yeah, Norm. Okay. Don't worry."

They say Mrs. Baumgartner fainted after we went by, taking the whole grapefruit pyramid down with her. Boy, I sure wish I'd turned around to see that.

I remember sitting in the back seat of a car between Dad and the doctor. The grinder was on my lap, weighing me down, but my hand still didn't hurt. "Dad?"

"What, Norman?"

"Ray can't make more chopped meat because we took the grinder."

"It doesn't matter, Norm. Just rest."

"Okay." I sank back into a fuzzy mist. Dr. Cupernail was listening to my heart again.

Then I suddenly remembered about the fireworks and how Mom always said I'd blow my hand off. Here I'd gone and lost my hand in the stupid meat grinder. I didn't have to wait for them to give me the bad news at the hospital. I knew I wasn't going to have a left hand when this was over. I started to laugh.

Dad put his hand on my shoulder. "Norm, what's the matter?"

"It wasn't the fireworks, like Mom thought."

"What?"

"The hand. I never got near Leon's fireworks, but it's gone anyway."

"He's not making any sense," Dad said.

Dr. Cupernail nodded as he folded up his stethoscope. "Shock," he whispered.

But I was making sense in my own head. It's like the old saying that you'll die when it's your time to go. Well, me and my left hand had two different times to go. If I hadn't lost that hand in the meat grinder, it would have gotten blown off by Leon's fireworks for sure. No matter how far away from him I stood, one of those darn rockets would have aimed itself right at me.

Even in my foggy state, it all became perfectly clear. When I came into this world, my left hand had a return-trip ticket for July 4, 1946. I was just glad the rest of me wasn't going back to heaven with the hand.

I would have explained my theory to Dad and Dr. Cupernail, but that's when I passed out.

ALSO AVAILABLE
FROM SQUARE FISH BOOKS

If you like sports, you'll love these SQUARE FISH sports books!

Airball • L. D. Harkrader
ISBN-13: 978-0-312-37382-5 • $6.99 U.S./$7.99 Can.
"Even non-basketball fans will savor the on-court action and will cheer loudly for these determined players." —*Publishers Weekly*

Busted! • Betty Hicks
ISBN-13: 978-0-312-38053-3 • $6.99 U.S./$7.99 Can.
"Soccer fans will appreciate the exciting game action....A winning combination of sports and humor." —*School Library Journal*

Getting in the Game • Dawn FitzGerald
ISBN-13: 978-0-312-37753-3 • $6.99 U.S./$8.99 Can.
"Fast and funny...and readers who are caught up by the sports will stay around for the family and friendship drama." —*Booklist*

Soccer Chick Rules • Dawn FitzGerald
ISBN-13: 978-0-312-37662-8 • $6.99 U.S./$8.99 Can.
"An expression of the sheer joy of athletic competition and the hard-breathing fray of the game." —*Kirkus Reviews*

SQUARE FISH
WWW.SQUAREFISHBOOKS.COM
AVAILABLE WHEREVER BOOKS ARE SOLD